32.790
7/97
"A

MOULTONBORO LIBRARY

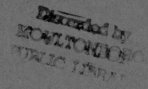

DATE DUE

"Hello," I Lied

a novel by

M. E. KERR

HarperCollinsPublishers

Library of Congress Cataloging-in-Publication Data

Kerr, M. E.

    "Hello," I lied : a novel / by M. E. Kerr

      p.   cm.

    Summary: Summering in the Hamptons on the estate of a famous rock star, seventeen-year-old Lang tries to decide how to tell his longtime friends that he is gay, while struggling with an unexpected infatuation with a girl from France.

    ISBN 0-06-027529-4. — ISBN 0-06-027530-8 (lib. bdg.)

    [1. Homosexuality—Fiction.   2. Bisexuality—Fiction.   3. Rock music—Fiction.]   I. Title.

PZ7.K46825He   1997   96-44132

[Fic]—dc20   CIP

                                      AC

Typography by Steve M. Scott

1   2   3   4   5   6   7   8   9   10

❖

First Edition

For Bill Morris,

there from the very beginning,

cheerful companion on the road,

with thanks and love

ONE

Some people said I'd never see him. Very few had seen him in ten years. That was when he quit playing, writing, performing—quit everything. Retired at thirty-two. Not burned out like some rockers. Just finished.

Ben Nevada was a star like Elvis, John Lennon, Dylan, or Mick Jagger. Even if he wasn't around anymore, the name would be, the fame would be. He said it himself in "Flame."

> *Let the fame go,*
> *Let the game go,*
> *But the flame glows,*
> *And the fire grows,*
> *I'm a fire!*

❖

We moved to Roundelay on Memorial Day weekend. You couldn't even see his house from ours, although we were at the same address.

We had the caretaker's cottage. It was down by the road near the gate, where the rottweilers lunged against the fence with their teeth bared, five of them, wearing red collars with silver spikes.

He'd never named them. He had a theory that if you named something, you grew fond of it. If you got fond of dogs, next thing you brought them

1

into your house. He didn't want them in there. He already had three house dogs, all of them chows.

The rottweilers weren't pets. They were guards. He called them A, B, C, D, and E. He fed them himself. He drove down in his black Range Rover and tossed chunks of beef into their bowls. "Eat up!" he'd snarl at them. That was so they knew he was their master. He didn't scratch their ears, pet them, or let them walk with him. He just watched them eat.

He knew A was the fat one, and C was the one who waited for the others to eat before he would. He knew their ways. But he saved his affection for the chows.

I'd been told all that by Franklin, the houseman.

"If you see him feeding the dogs, just take off. You probably won't be up that early, anyway, but if you ever are, get lost!"

Of course, I saw him all the time on tape.

I'll never forget the first time.

Remember "Night in the Sun"? Remember his entrance?

He came out wearing black leather thigh-high boots, red silk jockey shorts, and a long black leather trenchcoat. He wore a big gold star on a gold chain around his neck. Backing him up was his killer band: Bobby Dale on guitar, the Matero twins on keyboards. I can't remember who was on bass, but Twist was on drums.

The song lasted five minutes and ended with him

down on his knees, leaning backward all the way to the floor on this darkened stage with the overhead spotlight focused on him.

I never saw anything like it.

Even if I hadn't been a rock fan, I would have remembered that performance. You don't have to know anything about rock to be moved by it. All you need is eyes and ears and some connection with the human race. If you never had a heart, you grew one, listening to that husky voice wrenching out the words.

You wondered how he could put all that out there, come up with those moves, tap into everything you never knew was buried deep inside you. You wondered if he knew what he was causing you to feel, if he cared or didn't care, if he was aiming at you or just letting go some wild stuff he couldn't hold back if he wanted to.

The audience went crazy.

Even on tape you could feel yourself part of it. I almost cried. I did laugh. Hard. It was the first time I ever understood the pull of a Jesus or a Hitler. First time I ever knew what made people scream when a Magic ran out on the basketball court, or a Martina whacked a tennis ball across the net. . . . It made me appreciate what got into groupies, fans, worshippers, and followers.

So it was Ben Nevada who gave me my first real taste of charisma.

You can imagine how I felt when Mom told me who she was going to work for that summer.

I was seventeen going on eighteen.

After school was over in New York, I'd be living there full-time, too.

I was going to help out, do odd jobs, and five nights a week I'd be a waiter at Sob Story on the Montauk Highway.

Help out, hide out, cool out, come out—all four things at once.

That was the trouble that summer.

About all I was sure of was my name: Lang Penner.

T W O

"*What's* your name? Lane?"

"No, sir. *Lang*."

"Kind of a name is that?" he barked.

He stood on the dunes scowling down at me.

"Lang was my mother's maiden name," I said.

"Are you Lucy's son?"

"Yes, sir."

"Don't you know you're not supposed to be down here?"

"I'm not supposed to be on the beach?"

"This is *my* beach!"

"I didn't know that, sir."

"This is the second time I've seen you down here."

"Yes, sir. When we first moved in, I walked down here with a friend."

"Walk down there." He waved his hand at the beach farther down. He had two chows at his feet.

"Well, you're here now, aren't you?" he said. "Go fetch my other dog." He tossed me a red leather lead. "You'll need this. Plato is stubborn. He knows we're heading back to the house."

Some house. It was about 20,000 square feet. That early-summer morning it looked like a whole kingdom sifting into sight through the fog.

I whistled at the dog sitting in the sand, his black

5

tongue out as he panted. Once Alex had owned a chow. I remembered him telling me they were the only dogs who didn't have pink tongues.

Then I called, "C'mon, boy!"

Nevada snapped, "No! You have to go and get him! Plato doesn't follow orders. He's like you."

"Nobody gave me any orders," I mumbled.

I was carrying two paperbacks. I went down to the chow, hooked the lead on him, and led him back to where Nevada was waiting for me.

"What do you mean, nobody gave you any orders?" he asked me. "Everything's printed out on the sheet I gave your mother. Didn't you bother to read it?"

"I read it. I guess I didn't understand it."

"Didn't understand it," he said in a crabby tone.

"I *didn't!*" I protested.

"I heard you."

I walked behind him for a while. He wasn't at all what I'd expected. He was taller and somehow more dignified and well-spoken. There were silver streaks through his thick black hair, and his jeans were pressed and creased. He had on a black T-shirt and black leather thong sandals, and the only jewelry was a large gold watch with a black face. I did some fast addition. He was forty-two. He looked older. He had a tan and the wrinkles around his eyes that go with people who spend a lot of time outdoors.

He turned around and waited for me to catch up with him.

Plato was tugging hard on the lead, but the other two chows heeled nicely, stopped when he did, looked up at him, waiting for the next move.

"What are you doing down on the beach at seven in the morning?" he asked me.

"Walking. Reading." I had always gotten up early in New York, just as soon as the garbage men began rattling the cans outside our apartment windows.

"What are you reading?" he asked me.

"Just some novels."

"What are they?"

"One is a book by Edmund White," I said. "The other one's by Truman Capote." I wished I had butchier reading material: an Elmore Leonard, or even a Stephen King. But I was trying to read stuff Alex liked. He was a big reader, and I was trying to catch up with him.

"Capote?" Nevada said.

"Yes."

"A fairy."

"Yes."

I waited for him to vent, wisecrack, whatever.

He said, "Like Elton John."

"Yeah."

"He wrote one song I wished I'd written. 'Yellow Brick Road.' You know that song?"

"Yes, sir."

"Don't keep saying 'Yes, sir.' You can say 'Yes, Mr. Nevada.'"

"All right . . . Mr. Nevada."

We walked along while the fog began lifting, showing more of Roundelay.

I asked him why he'd named his house that.

"Don't you know what a roundelay is?" he said.

"Not really."

"It's a simple song, with a phrase or a line repeated."

"My mother thought it was a dance."

"It is. That too," he said.

The chows trotted along beside us, Plato still struggling to go faster.

Nevada said, "If you had to describe yourself using only one word, what would that word be?"

"What?" I'd heard him, but the question was so out of the blue, it threw me.

He repeated it, looking down at me with his dark-blue eyes, frowning.

I thought of Alex. I thought of the way he smelled of patchouli sometimes first thing in the morning. I thought of Brittany, too, of how she'd complain, "You don't know how to kiss, do you?"

I said, "Torn."

"Torn?" he bellowed.

"Sometimes."

"Torn between what and what?" he demanded.

"Torn between comfort and conformity."

What was I doing spilling out my guts to *him*?

He said, "My father used to say, 'First do what is

expected of you! Then enjoy the surprise of finding out you like it.'"

"Uh-huh."

"They fuck us up!" he said.

"What?" I wasn't sure I'd heard him right.

"Parents," he said. "That's from a poem by Philip Larkin."

He stopped in his tracks, tossed his head back, and quoted the whole thing.

It was a real blast against family.

Later, I would learn he liked to quote from Shakespeare, the Bible, Yeats, Auden—all writers you wouldn't figure he'd ever read.

Later, I would come to know he regretted never going to college, never having a decent education.

It was his Achilles' heel.

But that hot, muggy day in June, with the sun already making us both perspire, I just kept trying to put this man together with the fellow in black leather, on his knees, leaning so far back you wondered how anyone could bend a body like that, thrusting his pelvis skyward while the drums and bass played the same lick over and over, and the audience almost crazy.

"That poem is called 'This Be the Verse,'" he said.

I vaguely remembered he had some quarrel with his father, that it was all through his music. Something about his old man never letting go of him, always controlling him.

We walked along silently with the chows until Roundelay stretched before us in all its glory.

There was a fork in the path.

He stopped long enough to take Plato's lead from me.

"I don't want to see you on my beach again, Lane," he said.

"It's *Lang*, Mr. Nevada."

He gave me a little two-fingered salute, no smile.

He headed toward Roundelay and I took the other path.

THREE

"How's everything at Manderley?" Alex asked. That's what he called Roundelay. It was the name of the house in *Rebecca*, an old movie we both liked, with Judith Anderson playing the evil Mrs. Danvers.

Last night I dreamt I went to Manderley again—that was the opening line.

I told him I'd met Ben Nevada, and how he'd asked me to describe myself in one word.

I didn't tell Alex I'd answered "torn." I told him I'd said "content."

"How would *you* describe yourself in one word?" I said.

"Envious."

I laughed. "I'll probably never see him again."

"If you do, ask him why Cali always said, 'Pain over!' at the end of every song."

"Oh, sure. I'm going to bring *her* name up!"

"It's been years since she died."

"Fourteen years exactly," I said.

Right after my encounter with Nevada that morning, I went down to the library. I did a little research with the help of the computer there, surfing through old news stories. One I printed out.

**EX-ROCK SINGER DEAD IN CRASH:
CALI COSS, AGE 26**

Cali Coss was among the dead in yesterday's crash of the Boeing 707, along with her husband, Leonard Haun. After skyrocketing to fame with Ben Nevada's band, then plummeting into a life of drug abuse, she recovered in her two-year marriage to Haun, an insurance executive.

There was more about her upbringing in a poor family in Kentucky, and about the songs said to be inspired by her, written by Nevada.

There was a photograph of her, a poor reproduction of her singing at a concert in Japan.

I'd never heard her sing, but I'd heard that Nevada wrote his famous song "Heart in My Mouth" about her.

"She's the reason he doesn't perform anymore," Alex said.

"She'd already left him. He still gave concerts after she left him."

"But he never got over her," Alex said. "Didn't you ever hear 'You Took Me with You' or 'Tell Me Where You Are So I Know Where I Am'?"

I didn't keep up on star gossip the way Alex did.

Then he reminded me the call was costing him money and we started making our weekend plans.

"You come in, okay?" he said. "We have a benefit on Sunday night. When you finish at Sob Story Saturday, hitch a ride in and we'll have until late Sunday afternoon."

Alex was playing Fortinbras in *Hamlet.*

He wasn't just playing Fortinbras. He was also a soldier in one scene and a messenger in another. But it was his very first speaking role on Broadway. And it was Shakespeare again. Usually when he did Shakespeare, he was little more than a spear carrier.

We made arrangements for me to pick up a pizza and meet him at his apartment after the show.

I never went backstage. Even though Alex was "out" everywhere, I wasn't. And I didn't think it did him any good to have me showing up at the theater.

One time he'd played the hunk in *Picnic* in some amateur summer theater production. The actress starring with him blamed a bad review on Alex. Some small-town drama critic wrote that she was "wooden." She claimed she couldn't work up any emotion playing opposite a boy who preferred other boys to girls.

Alex laughed it off. He said, "When the lady doesn't know how to dance, she says the musicians don't know how to play."

But I never forgot him telling me about it, and I wouldn't hang around backstage for everyone to gape at me.

After I hung up, I went out to the kitchen, where Mom was making fried chicken for Nevada and his guests that night.

Nevada couldn't stand cooking smells in Roundelay,

so Mom made most meals in our cottage. Then Franklin would drive down in the Range Rover and pick everything up.

That was just fine with Mom. She said he played music full blast over the sound system, and as huge as Roundelay was, he had speakers in every room and insisted that all of them be on. If it wasn't music, it was his French language tapes. He wanted to learn French for some mysterious visitor he was expecting that month.

"Bonjour, madame," I said. *"Comment allez-vous?"*

"Don't," she said. "I hear enough of that up there."

"Alex sends his love."

"Poor Alex in that hot city all summer!"

"Alex loves New York, Mom."

"Does he have air conditioning?"

"In that dump on Avenue A? It'd blow all the fuses."

I sat down and watched her. She could cook a four-course dinner for twelve and look as unruffled and neat as a clubwoman after a few rounds of bridge. Even her apron was spotless.

We were both blond and green eyed, but I had my father's height, she said, and she hoped that was all I'd inherited from him. Any information I had concerning him was secondhand. He'd taken off before I'd learned to walk. The only photograph I had of him was taken outside a place in Las Vegas called Circus Circus. Mom liked to say it was snapped during one of the rare moments when he wasn't *inside* a casino. He was a gambler—a grinning, lanky fellow wearing a black, open-collared shirt, white pants, and a belt with a big silver buckle.

Mom had been born in Atlantic City, and when the card players and one-armed bandits took over, she got a job at The Golden Nugget. Met him there, fell in love, married him.

Last we heard of him, he was running the roulette wheel on some ship, specializing in Caribbean cruises.

"I've been thinking about that word game Mr. Nevada played with you," she said.

"Played *on* me," I said. "He didn't say what word described him."

"I'm glad you said 'torn,' Lang."

"Not about being gay, Mom. About coming out. Sometimes I feel as though I'm living this lie. Other times I feel I should just keep my mouth shut."

"I'm glad you told me, but I don't see why it has to be anybody else's business. . . . And I still think it's too soon for you to make up your mind about being gay."

"How old were *you* when you made up your mind you were straight?"

She sighed and said, "All right. I don't have time for one of your gay pride lectures, honey. I have to finish this chicken. Can you lend a hand?"

While we were loading up the tray, I said, "What word would you use to describe yourself?"

She came up with the same word I'd told Alex I'd answered. *Content.*

"Mr. Nevada is paying me more than I ever got before, for doing something I love doing . . . and you're included. That's contentment," she said. "And I'm happy. Is that the same thing as content?'

"I'd say it's synonymous."

"So be it," she said. "All goes well."

I could look out the window and see the dandelions in the field, where Franklin had warned us there were sometimes snakes.

At the end of that summer I often thought about that moment.

The flower heads had turned into the white golf-ball-sized bunches of seeds that floated about in the wind like tiny parachutes. Gliding under them, unseen, were the long lengths slipping out in the sun for some warmth before they sneaked back into their crevices.

Fluff flying above the mysteries beneath them.

My mother and I, content, happy. What we couldn't see was all around us, but it was hidden, waiting to surprise us if we moved in its direction.

And we would.

FOUR

Before Alex I'd never been in a relationship, never worried about looking faggy, even though when I was a kid I was this dizzy sissy who played with dolls and screamed at spiders. I outgrew all that, butched up and worked out, so when the two of us got together, little things would remind me of what I used to be like. Alex loved stuff like Ice Blue Shampoo from The Body Shop, and smelly soaps from the Gap. I got to like them, too, but I thought they were too faggy to buy and bring home, so I wouldn't.

Alex would sometimes cry in movies, but I'd look away during sad parts and think of things to take my mind off what I was watching, because I didn't want to seem faggy.

Alex liked ballet and I hated going with him, even though I liked it too. I'd look around at all the guys there two by two and want to die.

Alex liked to cook, and he grew purple globe basil and Italian parsley on his windowsill. I'd tease him, tell him anyone down in the street could look up and know a fag probably lived there.

That was how we landed up at Adieu, Adieu in the East Sixties last April. We were celebrating Alex's first speaking role on Broadway.

We'd pooled our money to splurge on a good dinner.

Alex said there were plenty of great gay restaurants we could go to, but I didn't even want to be seen going into one of those places. So he let me choose.

I read this write-up in *The New York Times* about this French place hidden away in a little brownstone.

Alex's dad was a chef. Not just a cook like Mom, but a gourmet, and he'd taught Alex about food. Thanks to Alex, I learned there was a whole world beyond steak and mashed, my favorite meal when I was a kid.

We ordered escargots, which I tried to forget were snails, and we were going to follow that with wild boar stew.

After the waiter took our orders, I told Alex that I'd finally come out to Mom.

"Well, what did she say?"

"She said she'd been waiting for me to show some real interest in girls, and when I didn't she thought I might just be developing slowly."

"Like a photograph taken with an old Polaroid." Alex chuckled.

"Then I began bringing you home."

"That fairy actor."

"She *likes* you."

"But I blew your scene, right?"

"No. She'd just never known me to be that attached to anyone. It wasn't anything about *you*. It was the way I acted around you. She said it was worlds away from how I acted around Brittany."

"Was she upset?"

"More philosophical than upset. She said it was a hard life."

"If you're lucky," Alex cracked.

"She asked me when I first knew about myself."

"When did you?"

"I saw some show on TV. Some father telling his son he was gay. I knew that night."

"I saw that show. But I knew already."

"I sat in front of the TV shaking."

"Poor baby. Afraid?"

"Afraid and relieved. I was just a kid: seven, eight? Before that I knew something was wrong with me. It didn't even have to do with sex."

Alex grinned. "I know. I was always upstairs in my room dancing around to *Hello, Dolly!* or *Gypsy*. The other guys were all off to the ballpark."

When the waiter brought us our whiskey sours, minus the whiskey, we clinked our glasses together.

"Here's looking at us!" Alex said.

"To us!"

Alex told me about the first time he'd ever had wild boar. His father had introduced it to him when the family took a trip to France. He said that trip, when he was fifteen, was the last happy family experience he'd had. While he was showering in the hotel room, his twin brother, Peter, read an unfinished letter he'd left on the desk. It was to another boy, telling him how he missed him, saying all he did was wish they could be in Paris together because Paris was filled with lovers.

And Alex's twin had always been envious of him because even as a kid Alex had worked on stage and made some commercials.

He told their mother, so when they got back to the States, she took Alex to see a psychiatrist. His father blamed himself for bringing home so many "nellie chefs"—a lot of his father's colleagues were closet gays.

"They kept blaming themselves, blaming each other, then blaming my shrink, who said I didn't seem to have as big a problem with it as they did."

"And now?" I said.

"You met them. They're resigned to it, but not delighted. Peter hates it. He's afraid people will think he's one of us."

"Your father never gets my name right. He calls me Lynn."

We hadn't been paying much attention to anything going on around us. We were new to each other. We had a lot of catching up to do.

You notice Alex, though. Everywhere we went, people took a second look at him. He's even taller than I am, and he's got this great face. He has the kind of looks a Brad Pitt has, or a Jason Priestly.

I finally saw a woman at a center-row table watching us. Not watching us: staring at us. She was with this heavyset loudmouth I figured she was embarrassed by, because you could tell he'd been drinking. He was doing all the talking, and she kept looking our way . . . at Alex, I thought. And I thought: Eat your heart out!

Because I liked having people admire him, liked knowing he was really something . . . and he was with *me*.

Maybe the fellow with her was watching us in the mirror. The restaurant walls were all mirrored. Maybe she said something to him.

He was paying the bill, and when the waiter took the money, the guy got up, glanced at us, and snarled something I couldn't hear.

Alex was a blusher. I saw his face get bright red.

I saw other people turn to look at us.

"What'd he say?" I asked Alex.

"Never mind. Let's not spoil the evening."

"But what'd he say, Alex?"

He was lumbering toward the door by then. The waiter was bowing and thanking him, and the maitre d' was smiling at him, telling him it was good to see him again.

Alex said, "He said, 'Your kind doesn't belong in a place like this.'"

"What?" I couldn't believe it. "What'd we do?"

Alex kept his voice low. "We're the only two guys together here. Saturday night. We were laughing, clinking glasses. How the hell do *I* know?"

"He's gone," I said. "You're right. Let's not let anything spoil this."

"We're ready for the check, anyway," said Alex.

We tried to get past it. I was in shock. We talked about why Alex loved doing Shakespeare, and what was wrong with me that I didn't really appreciate the plays.

21

"Ignorance is what's wrong with me," I said.

Alex said, "You just don't give it a chance. You'd *love* it if you got into it, Lang. I know you would."

"Nothing seems to grab me that way," I said. "I keep thinking I'd like to be a writer, but I hardly read at all."

"You love films."

"I love *movies*," I said. "Why do you say 'films'?"

"Why not?" He shrugged.

"It sounds a little affected," I said.

He said, "That guy got to you, didn't he?"

"Are you *kidding*?" I said, but he was right. He knew he was too.

"Don't let things like that stick with you, Lang," he said. "It's always going to happen somewhere, at some point, usually when you least expect it."

"Okay."

He was only three years older than I was, but sometimes I felt as though he was a decade older. I knew he was more sophisticated, better educated. He'd gone to prep school; he'd traveled a lot more than I had. . . . And he had his own apartment, never mind that it was a rat hole. He wasn't still trying to figure out what to do with his life.

I wondered if the loudmouth had said something to the waiter and the maitre d'. I noticed we weren't thanked or smiled at as we left the restaurant.

"Did you feel a chill back there?" I asked Alex as we

headed toward the parking lot next door.

"It was a little cool, for sure," he said.

It was the last Saturday night we'd have together. Alex would be working the following week.

The stars were out. The air had that balmy early-spring feeling. We were going to go back to Alex's place and watch an old Marlon Brando picture: *On the Waterfront*.

It would be the last time Alex had his mother's neat little Volkswagen convertible, too. She'd decided owning a car in the city was too much trouble.

As we walked toward the Volks, I said, "Hey, it's warm enough to put the top down."

"You think so?" Alex said.

I remember the grin on his face as he looked down at me. I remember him giving me a wink.

Then suddenly we saw the loudmouth pull up in a black Chrysler. He had the window rolled down, and he called out, "Faggots!"

Alex laughed and called back, "We're here, we're queer, get used to it!"

It was something people chanted in gay marches.

That was all it took to make the fellow brake, get out, and ask Alex if he wanted to repeat it.

"Keep going," I said to Alex, and we did.

He was following us, and Alex said, "There are two of us, so get ready, Lang, he might—"

And then he did.

Whatever he had in his hand—a tire iron, or one of

those iron bars that lock car steering wheels—came down on Alex's head hard.

Alex stumbled, and then the guy swung the thing a second time, so Alex fell.

It happened so fast that by the time I knelt down beside Alex, the fellow had run back to his car. The door slammed. The Chrysler took off just as another couple came into the lot to get their car.

"I saw the whole thing," a woman said. "I'll go back and call the police."

Her date said, "We'll get some help! He's bleeding."

The police wanted to know what it was all about.

"He didn't like the looks of us," Alex said.

I thought they'd say, "What do you mean, the *looks* of you?" but they seemed to know what he meant without asking.

The manager of Adieu, Adieu claimed that customer had never been in his restaurant before, had paid in cash, had no reservation. He said he didn't know him or the woman with him.

"In a pig's eye!" Alex muttered as we drove down First Avenue. We were headed for the emergency room at St. Vincent's Hospital.

He'd barely managed to get himself behind the wheel of the Volks. He was bleeding and bruised.

"I wasn't much help," I said.

"At least you had the sense to keep your mouth

shut. I was the one who waved the red flag at the bull."

"But I wish he'd swung at me. I don't have to be onstage in a week."

Alex said, "Enter Fortinbras . . . limping."

FIVE

"Lang? It's Brittany."

"Where are you?"

"In Sag Harbor. Nick and I are visiting Allie Perez. We're going on a picnic over in East Hampton at Main Beach—Allie, me, and Nick. Want to come along?"

"I'd like to see Nick."

"Oh, *thanks*."

"I just don't want to start up again, Brittany."

"Who *does*? That's past history."

Back before I met Alex, we'd dated for a while. She used to joke and say we were "lover," because only one of us was ever involved.

I said, "What'll I bring?"

"Just yourself. Allie made enough ribs and potato salad for an army. We'll pick you up at noon. Just give me directions."

I told her the number on Ocean Road and said I'd be out front.

Nick was a buddy, way before I ever went out with his sister. We grew up in the same neighborhood, and though he was ahead of me in school, we hung out together. I'd given him my phone number when he told me Allie's folks had a summer place in the Hamptons, but I'd never expected he'd call.

26

Nick and Allie had one of these on again/off again relationships that was mostly off. Allie liked to date other guys, and Nick was so crazy about her, he'd explode when she went out with someone else. Then they wouldn't speak for weeks. Then they would. I never really thought of them as a couple. I'd complain to Nick about their fighting in front of me, tell him what a bore that was.

Mom said, "Did you tell him not to drive up to the gate?"

"I'll be down there at ten to twelve," I said.

It had been two days since my encounter with Nevada. I hadn't even told Nick who Mom was working for. She didn't think it was right to give out his address.

"If you tell them Mr. Nevada lives here, be sure to warn them that it's private information," Mom said.

"I will. They're cool."

I changed my clothes, grabbed some paperbacks from my stash, and tucked them into my knapsack with a towel and some suntan lotion.

Then I headed down to the gate, fifteen minutes ahead of schedule, just to be sure.

I was standing there about five minutes when Franklin appeared in the Range Rover.

The rottweilers were up on their hind legs snarling

and barking, so Franklin had to shout to be heard.

"What're you doing, Lang?"

He didn't need the dogs to alert him. The security cameras at Roundelay were always on.

I explained that I was waiting for a ride, and he began shaking his head even before I'd finished.

"Mr. Nevada doesn't want anyone loafing around here, Lang."

"I didn't think I was in camera range."

"Everything is. Wait down the road a piece."

"How far down?"

"See that line of oak trees?"

"Way down there?"

"Way down there," he said. "Mr. Nevada is getting ready to leave too. Don't let him catch you this close."

Nick was late.

I stood there in the hot sun, waiting.

About five minutes after twelve an old Ford roadster paused by the gate on its way from Roundelay.

It looked like something out of the thirties. Whitewall tires with wire wheels. Black with a white canvas top. Pinstriping going the length of the car back to the rumble seat. Running boards and a spare tire attached to the rear.

I knew Nevada was behind the wheel. I saw he was wearing a black cap. I turned my back on him so he wouldn't think I was watching him.

He just sat there in the thing.

Another five minutes and Nick appeared in a dark-green Saturn, going slow. I got out in the middle of the road and waved my hands, and he came up to me and stopped.

One of the side doors opened, and Brittany said, "Hi! Hop in."

As we headed away, I looked through the rear window and saw Nevada following us.

"Did you see that car?" Nick said. "It's a thirty-four Ford! It's a classic!"

"It's no secret who lives there," Allie said as we stretched out on Main Beach. "Out here we know where all the celebrities live. Nobody bothers them."

"What's he like, Lang?" Nick asked me.

I told him about the one time I'd run into him by accident.

"He bought that place for Cali Coss," Brittany said.

"'Pained over it,'" Allie said. "Wasn't that what she always said?"

"I thought it was 'Pain's over,'" Nick said.

We didn't talk about them long.

They asked me about Sob Story. It was popular with kids because weekend nights after the kitchen closed, they featured hot new groups like The Failures. They were already booked. Brittany said she'd kill for tickets to see Cog Wheeler, Failures' top dog. ("Hint hint," she said, nudging me.)

Nick and Allie began slathering each other with suntan lotion, giggling and cooing to one another, and Brittany turned over on her stomach with her face down in her arms.

I took out a copy of *Understanding Shakespeare* and tried to concentrate on it.

Then Nick and Allie went off to be alone together, and I switched to lighter reading, a Michael Nava mystery featuring his gay lawyer, Henry Rios.

When Brittany came awake, she flipped over to her back and asked me if I knew the words to any of Nevada's songs. She said he was a real poet.

I said I only knew the ones to "Flame."

"'I'm a fire.' Oh, yes."

"I probably know others, but never knew he wrote them. I've heard a lot about 'Heart in My Mouth.'"

"My favorite," she said. "Do you know the words?"

"I just said I didn't."

"Don't! Please! Don't get that tone, Lang!"

"I'm sorry."

"You seem to be always right on the edge with me."

"I'm not on the edge!"

"You should hear yourself. What is it with you?"

"It isn't anything. . . . How does 'Heart in My Mouth' go?"

I thought she'd probably recite the words, but she just sat up straight and began singing.

I'd never heard her voice, never knew anyone that good who didn't want to be a singer.

"You in my eyes bring my heart
To my mouth, bring the words
To my lips, feel my blood start
To race, singing of birds,
With the lifting of wings,
Heart in my mouth, spilling out things."

I clapped.

"You have to like Nevada," she said. "Someone who can write a song like that."

"How about someone who can sing a song like that?"

"Thanks, Lang."

I noticed some people on nearby blankets watching us. They were smiling. One boy put his hand up with the thumb and first finger making a circle.

"I guess they think I was singing you a love song," Brittany said. "I would if you could get me in to see Cog Wheeler. Aren't they playing at Sob Story in July?"

"I work in the kitchen, Brittany."

I was thinking, What if it had been Alex singing to me? And I was remembering the night at Adieu, Adieu.

Coming toward us on the beach, arms wrapped around each other, Nick and Allie stopped to kiss.

"Do you miss me at all, Lang?" Brittany asked me.

"It's just easier without you."

"*What* is?" She sounded really angry.

"My peace of mind. My goddamn life!" I snapped.

Allie had come back to the blanket with Nick.

"Oh, I hate couples who argue, don't you, Nick?"

"I *hate* it!" Nick said. "It's such a bore!"

That night at Sob Story I had a sunburn and a new duty. All the wine they sold arrived in the kind of waxed-cardboard containers milk comes in. I had to funnel it into empty bottles with fancy French labels and lug them out to the bar. That was what customers got when they ordered Merlot or Chablis for seven dollars a glass.

SIX

I'd first met Alex on a cold January day in Barnes & Noble, at 22nd and Sixth Avenue. I'd never been in that bookstore before, but Alex spent many hours a week there. It wasn't like any bookstore I'd ever seen. There were easy chairs all over, desks you could work at, even an upstairs espresso bar.

I'd gone there to listen to a new George Michael CD. Alex usually sat in the music section. We struck up a conversation, and he handed me a headset and told me to listen. It was an Elvis Costello song—"Almost Blue"—sung in this strange, husky voice Alex said was an old jazz singer named Chet Baker.

After that we sat there talking and drinking espresso. When I got to know him, I got to know places in New York I'd never heard of. Even though Alex's apartment on Avenue A was a dump, he made up for it by finding great places to hang out all over the city— Roosevelt Island, for one.

We headed there that Sunday I was in from East Hampton.

It is smack in the middle of the East River. We caught a tram on Second Avenue between East 59th and 60th. Then we took one of the old red buses out to Lighthouse Park.

We had a picnic there, thumbed through the

Sunday *Times*, and played chess. I think chess was the only thing I ever taught Alex.

Before we headed back, we took a walk on the island's west side, to get a view of the Manhattan skyline.

That was when we ran into Scott Lund.

He was walking ahead of us. I'd noticed him before Alex called his name. He had a white shirt on, buttoned at the wrists, with a polka-dot silk scarf under it. Something about him—everything about him, from his walk to his tight, tight pants—made me know he was gay. But he had his arm around a woman in a red dress, and he was bending down to kiss her, while she gave him this adoring look.

I was just about to whisper to Alex, "Get *her*!"—and I wouldn't have meant the lady in red.

"Scotty!" Alex called out to him.

"Alex! Alex Southgate! Come say hello to Maggie!"

He waited for us to catch up.

Alex introduced me, and we stood there chatting for a while.

He was an actor too, a lot older than Alex, starring in a Pinter revival that summer.

"Of all places to run into each other!" Scott gave Alex a friendly slap on the arm. "I'll tell Zack I saw you, Alex. Delighted to meet you, Lang!"

After we left them, Alex said, "That's his beard. He never goes anyplace without her."

"What's a beard?"

"She's his disguise. With her, he passes as straight."

"Oh, sure. And I'm Dolly Parton."

"He tries, poor old Scotty. She lives across the hall from Zack and him. I don't think I've ever seen Scotty with Zack in public."

"What's in it for her?"

"Oh, she gets to be seen with a famous actor. I don't know, Lang. She's crazy about him."

"A fag hag." I'd heard there were females who glommed onto gay guys.

"I think Scotty adores her, too, in his way."

"I think Scotty adores looking straight . . . only he can't pull it off."

"Some old fairies cope that way. The theater used to be filled with them. Some even marry."

"In name only."

"Some. Some not. Some have children."

"But they're not really bisexual. I think people who claim to be bisexual just can't admit they're queer. It's easier to say you're bi. That makes you halfway straight."

"I know gays of both sexes who've had heterosexual affairs."

"Actors. Acting."

Alex said, "People. Loving. Everything isn't as black and white as you make it. You're gay and I'm gay, but look at someone like Madonna."

"She's omnisexual," I said.

Alex laughed.

I watched Scotty mince along in the distance. I knew that walk. I'd seen comedians imitate it, for laughs.

I said, "Scotty's the kind of fairy that ruins it for the rest of us."

"No, Lang. Guys like Scotty *got* ruined. They didn't do the ruining. People are the way they are because of the way things were in their day. . . . Look at your friend Nevada."

"What about him?"

"The druggy seventies did *him* in. All those young rock stars were on some kind of dope."

"Some of them still are."

"And some of *us* still swish around. Don't try to make everyone fit a mold. Wasn't that the gist of one of Nevada's songs?"

I shook my head. "Everybody knows his songs but me."

Alex said, "It goes:

> *"If you make yourself me*
> *Then I might set you free*
> *Then I might let you be*
> *Then you might let me see*
> *That you've turned into me.*

It's called 'Dad's Advice.'"

"I remember. 'If my lies you believe, Then I might let you breathe.'"

"His songs are filled with Daddy, when they're not about Cali."

"What else do you know about him?"

"Hey, I thought you didn't like my star gossip. It's too faggy, isn't it? Isn't that what you tell me?"

"This is different. I'm right there at his place."

Alex said, "Don't get blown away by the winds of Roundelay." He laughed. "Sounds like a song."

SEVEN

That night when I got in, my mother handed me a sealed envelope.

Printed up in the space for the return address, in gold letters, was:

B. L. N.
Roundelay
Ocean Road
East Hampton, New York 11937

My name was written across the front.

"Hurry up and open it!" my mother said.

B. L. N., again, in gold, at the top of thick cream-colored paper.

I read it aloud:

Lang,
> *Please come up to Roundelay tomorrow at noon.*
> *I'll give you lunch.*
> *Use the back walk leading to the terrace.*
> *I'll meet you out there.*

Ben Nevada

"I wonder what he wants," Mom said.

"We know what he doesn't want. He doesn't want me in the house."

Mom shrugged. "Why should he? I'm not in

Roundelay that much myself. . . . You had a phone call, too. Brittany's in Sag Harbor. She said she'd be up late tonight, to call her. The number's written down on the pad by the phone."

"She was just here a few days ago."

"So? It's a free country." Then my mother asked, "Does Nick know about you, honey?"

"I never told him, or Brittany."

"No need to broadcast it," she said. "How do you handle it at Sob Story?"

"I don't. That place isn't about truth. When anyone orders a sizzling steak, right before it leaves the kitchen I toss a piece of lard between the cold serving tray and the hot aluminum plate under the dish with the steak. Then the waiter hoists it up to his shoulder and delivers it sizzling!"

My mother laughed. "But your boss observes the Sabbath, give him that. How many places out here close on Sunday in season?"

"Right!" I said. "Cheat the customer but keep the Sabbath."

Then she said, "Who're Cog Wheeler and The Failures? Today Liz Smith's column said they were appearing at Sob Story July fifth."

"They're this rock group."

I remembered Brittany mentioning it; I remembered her habit of reading all the gossip columnists. I figured she was still trying to get tickets.

EIGHT

"Brittany? Cog Wheeler and The Failures are sold out."

"Oh, hi, Lang!"

I could tell by her voice she'd been asleep.

I said, "Mom said you'd be up late."

"I'm up. What time is it?"

"Ten thirty. I'll call you tomorrow."

"No, wait! This isn't about Cog Wheeler. Did you ever make sand casts?"

"Sand castles?"

"Sand *casts*. You use plaster of Paris and salt water. And sand too, of course." She laughed.

"I never have."

"You know, I'm taking a summer course at Arts and Crafts. I have to make an ob-jay, ob-jet—"

"Objet d'art," I said, to help her out. Brittany wanted to be an artist.

"That's it! I have to make one with sand in it that I can bring to class next week. . . . So this isn't a date or anything evil like that. I'd just like some input . . . and I don't know anyone out here."

"Where's Allie?"

"She's got a job. I'm alone all day and I have Mom's car this week. There's no real beach in Sag Harbor."

Before I could say anything, she jumped in with "I promise not to sing."

"If you sang, that would be a plus. I like the way you sing."

"I feel *awful* about singing on the beach that way! I don't know how I could have done that!"

"It was fine. Maybe if you'd sing everything you have to say, we'd get along."

"It's not *me*, Lang."

"So if it's me, why call me?"

"You want the truth?"

"Yes."

"I hate to go to the beach alone."

I had to laugh.

She said, "I feel conspicuous."

"I see."

"I could pick you up tomorrow."

"Not tomorrow."

"Tuesday? Same time? Same place?"

"Go a little past the driveway."

Brittany always got her way. I didn't know how to tell her no. Not that Brittany Ball ever took no for an answer, anyway.

NINE

We ate chicken salad on the 100-foot terrace overlooking the Atlantic Ocean.

Besides Plato, there were the other two chows: Aristotle and Socrates.

Before he played other rock groups, we listened to The Failures for a while. Nevada remarked that he'd read an interview with Cog Wheeler in *Rolling Stone*, and he liked the sound of him.

It was a hot, gray, windy day with big waves pounding the beach.

Nevada seemed to like to dress all in black: same jeans I'd seen on him before, same thong sandals, a black silk shirt billowing out in the breeze.

He didn't talk a lot, except to say what music he was playing sounded like what sixties music. The Orb sounded like Pink Floyd. Sonic Youth sounded like Velvet Underground. That sort of thing.

I didn't know that much about sixties music. I didn't have much to say.

Franklin came out with a pitcher of iced tea and refilled our glasses. He took away our empty dishes and put down a plate of chocolate chip cookies.

"These are from Barefoot Contessa," Nevada said. "They're hard. I don't like them soft."

"They're good," I said.

He smoked French cigarettes called Gitanes. He took one from a pack, lit it, and exhaled a stream of smoke.

"Have you got a girlfriend out here?" he asked me.

"No."

"In New York City?"

"No."

"I didn't think so."

I didn't know what to say to that, so I said nothing.

"Do you play tennis?" he said.

"Yes, I do."

"Good!"

"Why is that good?"

"All right," he said, looking full at me for the first time, his dark-blue eyes fixed on mine. "I'll tell you what this is all about."

He took another long drag from his cigarette. The chows were asleep under the table.

He said, "Old friends of mine—both artists—have asked a favor of me. They live in France, in a little town called Aniane. It's in the Languedoc region, a part they call Deep France. In other words, the sticks!"

He looked down at his cigarette a moment.

I looked out at the ocean, remembering the first weekend at Roundelay, when Alex and I walked along the beach. Besides chess, I'd never had anything to show him; he was always showing me things. Then I had East Hampton, a place that would be new to both of us. He loved the looks of it. I remember that first morning he just ran into the ocean and threw himself into these giant waves, then came out soaking wet with his hair down in his eyes, hugging me, no sunglasses. He'd lost them in the water.

Nevada continued. "They have this daughter. Huguette. That's what they call her. They got this damn fool idea to bring her up over there! They're Americans, but they didn't want to raise the child here. Thought she'd be safer there, better educated, all that expatriate rot about Europeans being superior to us!"

He paused to sip his tea.

Toni Braxton began singing over the speakers. I wondered if he'd say who *she* sounded like.

But he went on. "This child, this girl, is about your age. Seventeen." He looked across at me as if to confirm the fact.

I said, "I'll be eighteen in July."

"Huguette was brought up in this dinky little French town filled with grape growers and farmers. She went to school in the place. No more than fourteen hundred people, *peasants*, in the place. Most of them are hicks! Ordinary working people . . . Huguette's a young, smart, healthy, very attractive girl, and what was she supposed to do in a little fly-speck town for amusement? She fell in love. She has fallen madly in love. Who do you suppose she fell in love with?"

I shrugged. "A grape grower?"

"A grape *picker*," he said. "A local yokel who picks grapes. She is besotted with him!"

44

His shouting woke up Plato. The chow raised his head and peered up at me with worried eyes.

Nevada raved on. "Obsessed, besotted, head-over-heels in love! Surprise, surprise. What did they expect?" He didn't want an answer. "So what this child needs now is some exposure to the real world, to *peers*! They want to get her out of there, away from him! They're sending her here for the summer. She arrives tomorrow."

He looked into my eyes once again and said, "That's where you come in."

I sat there waiting for the other shoe to drop, while Toni Braxton sang, and Nevada interjected, "This singer is very much like Roberta Flack."

"I never heard of Roberta Flack," I told him.

"You two would probably get along," he said.

I knew he didn't mean Roberta Flack and me.

"Now, here's what I have in mind," he said, finally getting to the point. "I'd like you to help me out. Take her to a movie now and then. Play some tennis with her. Show her around the Hamptons. Give her a taste of *real* life. Introduce her to some intelligent young people! Of course, I'll reimburse you for any amount you spend."

He looked at me and I looked at him.

"Well?" he said.

"It's not a very good idea," I said. "I don't know anyone out here."

"You were with a group the other day. I saw you."

"They're from New York, Mr. Nevada."

"Then you and Huguette would be good company for each other. You'd like a tennis partner, wouldn't you? Someone to spend time with? And it's easier to meet people when you're with someone."

I could see myself getting into another situation where I'd have to lie and pretend I was someone I wasn't, so I just sat there shaking my head.

"She wouldn't be interested in *you*," he said, "if that's what's bothering you, Lane."

"Lang," I said.

"She's in love with this French field boy!"

"I have other commitments."

"You mean your work at Sob Story?"

"Things I do on weekends."

"Do them. You don't have to give up your weekends."

For a moment neither of us said anything. Then he rubbed his forehead with his hand and sighed. "I don't know how to say this," he said.

I had the idea he was going to tell me that I worked for him, and that this would be part of my job.

"Just say it," I told him.

"All right. I think I know why you're reluctant to do this, Lang."

Plato was on his feet, rubbing his nose against Nevada's pant leg.

I said, "Why?"

"I saw you with your *friend* down on the beach that day."

I thought Alex was the blusher, but I felt my own face get red.

Nevada said, "It looked to me like more than a friendship. And those books you had with you—Truman Capote—he was homosexual." He held his hand up before I could say anything. "I don't give a damn about that sort of thing! That's *your* business. . . . In fact, Lang, I think in this situation it's all to the good! I don't want some young kid getting ideas about Huguette. She's got enough baggage without that! All I want is for you to show her a good time. I'll pay for it!"

I kept shaking my head.

"Remember our first meeting, when you described yourself as 'torn'?"

"I'm not, though."

"You said it. I didn't."

"What I meant was I get tired of the masquerade."

"It's all right to have ambivalence."

"I don't have ambivalence about *that.* I have ambivalence about keeping it to myself."

"Oh, I know at your age you know everything there is to know about yourself. It's only when you're my age that you look back and see a stranger, and it was *you*! . . . I look back and see a stranger who was a fool! Always trying to impress a man who hated him!"

"Your father?"

"It doesn't matter."

We sat there in silence.

Then he said, "He was an accompanist. Beware of

understudies, accompanists, and ghostwriters! Their own dreams are put aside while someone else is featured!"

More silence as he sucked on his cigarette.

"In my case," he said, "those dreams were foisted off on *me*! I had to be the star he never would be. And I was never good enough, because he was never good enough!"

"I guess I was lucky," I said. "I don't know my father. I don't even know where he is."

But Nevada was not interested in my story.

He said, "I think you're lucky that I just made you this offer. Why not agree to it? Can't you enjoy yourself with a girl?"

"It isn't that."

"Drive her around—"

I cut him off. "I don't have a car!" I said.

"I have six!"

That spring I'd taken driver ed and gotten my license, but I hadn't had much practice driving.

"I'd like to help you out, sir," I said, "but I can't spend my summer in another masquerade."

"What do you mean another one?"

"That's all I've been doing all my life!"

He looked annoyed. My life wasn't the point. His was.

So I said, "If someone asked you to take out a gay man and show him a good time, how eager would *you* be to do it?"

"That's different!" he barked.

"Why is it?"

"It just is, Lang. . . . No one would ask someone to do that. What I'm asking you to do is put yourself in a perfectly normal situation."

"It wouldn't be a normal situation for me."

"It wouldn't be something you haven't done before, though."

"I've done it too many times."

"Once more won't kill you."

I said, "Thanks for lunch," and stood up.

Plato got up and ran over to jump against my legs.

"Down, Plato!" he shouted.

But he was right about Plato; Plato didn't follow orders.

"Think it over, Lang!" he called after me.

Plato trotted along with me until Nevada's tone became ominous.

"PLATO! PLATO! *PLA*-TO!"

The Beatles sang me out as I went down the walk at the side of the house. "Love Me Do."

I thought of Alex and of the three months ahead of us.

TEN

There was plaster of Paris all over everything: my shirt, jeans, arms, and legs—Brittany's bikini, her body, even some on her face.

But we had these hardened chunks of sand and plaster to show for it, and we'd managed to get through the afternoon without an argument.

Then, on the way home, in her mother's BMW, while WBEA was playing Deep Blue Something, Brittany said, "I always loved their old hit 'Breakfast at Tiffany's.'"

"Yeah. It was a good song."

"This pair who didn't have anything in common but that movie they both liked."

"I liked the movie too. What was her name? Audrey Hepburn. Sitting on the fire escape, playing her guitar, singing 'Moon River.'"

"If it was really her singing."

"I think it was."

"Sometimes in movies they dub those singing voices."

"I think it was her."

"I forgot what a movie buff you are, Lang."

"I'm going to miss that out here. All they have is U.A. crap. No revivals. No foreign stuff."

"But you go into New York some weekends, don't you?"

"Some," I said.

"Isn't your friend Alex in a play?"

"He's in *Hamlet*."

"Gawd, is *he* a hunk!"

"Yeah."

"I wouldn't mind meeting him."

"You met him that day we ran into you at Saks."

"I mean really meet him."

I didn't say anything. We'd stopped at The Red Horse so she could pick up some groceries, and we were crossing the Montauk Highway, headed south, where the houses got bigger and you could smell the ocean.

Brittany said, "With you out here this summer and me in the city, it would be nice to have someone I could hang out with."

"We wouldn't hang out together if I *was* there, anyway."

"You've made that clear."

"Then what's this 'with you out here this summer and me in the city' crap?"

"Lang, what *is* it with you? You don't want me but you get mad if I hint that I'd like to meet Alex."

"I'm not mad!"

"You're mad."

"You've met Alex. Call him up if you're so hot to see him!"

"You see? You'd hate it if I called him up!"

"Call him up and see how much I'd hate it!"

"I might."

"He's the one who'd hate it."

"Why would he hate it?"

"He wouldn't be interested."

"We'll see."

We were coming toward The Maidstone Club, which was the big-deal social snob scene, a block from Roundelay. Franklin had told my mother they'd turned Nevada down when he'd wanted to join so he could play golf there. They didn't like rock stars. They didn't like Jews or blacks, either. They didn't like more people than they did like.

"I *will* call him up," Brittany said. I thought she'd dropped it.

She said, "Just because you think I'm unattractive, that doesn't mean others don't find me attractive."

"I never said you were unattractive, Brittany."

"You said Alex wouldn't find me interesting."

"No. I said he wouldn't be interested."

"That's the same thing."

"No, it's not."

"Why isn't it the same thing?"

"Would you let me out here? I can walk from here."

I'd had it.

It was what always happened between us: bantering until it began boiling, then boiling over.

"Tell me the difference between not being interested and not finding someone interesting," she said.

I said, "Someone could be interesting, but if someone was gay, they might not be interested."

I could see the property marker for Roundelay, which was four acres away from where we were.

"Oh, Gawd, Lang, you'll really stoop to anything!" said Brittany.

I was thinking just a minute or two more and I'd be out of there.

Brittany said, "Are you trying to tell me Alex is gay?"

"Alex is. I am." My voice was very calm and suddenly so was I. Very calm.

I could feel her eyes on me. I kept looking straight ahead. Someone had to watch the road.

"You're gay?"

"I'm gay."

She said, "Then you and Alex are . . . ?"

She didn't finish.

"A couple." I helped her out.

We were right at that point near Roundelay where I had to get out, down by the oak trees, away from the gate.

She stopped the BMW.

I said, "That was what was wrong. Not you."

"Now you tell me."

"I should have told you before. I didn't know how."

"Damn right you should have told me before!"

"Well, I told you." I opened the door.

"Yes. Get out!" she said.

It was then that I saw Nevada's Ford heading out of the gate, turning in our direction.

I got out.

I shut the door.

"Lang?"

I turned around. The window on the passenger side was open.

Through it came one of the sand casts.

I jumped out of the way and it crashed on the pavement.

Then Brittany took off, the wheels squealing as she made a right turn too fast.

The Ford stopped in front of me.

Behind the wheel was a girl with short black hair and green eyes, grinning.

She leaned over and called out, "Hey! Who threw the brick at you?"

I'd picked up the two pieces of the sand cast I'd made.

I held them up. "It's not a brick."

"Rocks?" She laughed. "Someone threw rocks at you?"

I laughed too. "It's a long story."

"Get in!" she said. "Show me the way to town, hmmm?"

I leaned against the door. The window was rolled down. "I'm Huguette Haun," she said.

"I heard you were coming."

"So who are you?"

"Lang Penner." I thought of *Breakfast at Tiffany's*. She looked like her, like that actress Audrey Hepburn.

Only she spoke with a French accent. "Glad to meet you, Huguette."

"Eu, Eu, *Eu*gette," she said. "If you say my name *You*gette, you get nothing!"

She opened the car door for me.

"Get in!"

ELEVEN

Main Street in East Hampton was filled with places where you could pick up a pair of old bookends for $1,000, or a pair of jeans for $300.

My mother would come back to Roundelay with her eyes rolling in her head, quoting prices to me. She never bought anything.

Huguette parked in front of Polo, flashing a charge card she said "Uncle Ben" gave her. That was what she called Nevada. They weren't related, but she said he'd been in her life as long as she could remember, and he was like an uncle to her. "A rich one," she'd said.

Everyone did double takes when they saw us. The old Ford was part of it; the rest of it was her.

She was this beautiful girl with a sort of boisterous style and that foreign accent. She was wearing this sleeveless black shift, with a long slit in the back, tan sandals attached to these long legs, a huge, gold watch on her wrist, with gold bracelets dangling in front of it, gold hoop earrings, and this big, white smile.

When we'd go in any place, the clerks would look past me with plaster of Paris still spotting my jeans and my arms, and they'd head from behind their counters with open arms, ready to show her the Polos and the Guccis and the DKNYs.

She was looking for a white, heavy man's or

woman's terrycloth robe, which she couldn't find any-where. She said Uncle Ben had black ones and there was nothing more depressing than getting out of a hot shower and slipping into a big, black robe.

I told her there was a shopping center about five miles away, but she said she wanted to look around, anyway. She said she'd never had her own charge card, and money burrowed a hole in her pocket.

"Burns," I said.

"What?"

"Money *burns* a hole in your pocket."

"I never had any," she said.

"I still don't."

"You live here and you're poor?"

"My mother works for your uncle."

"Oh, you're the one."

"The one what?"

"The one who's supposed to show me the sights. Uncle Ben told me about you."

"When was that?"

"The other night when he called. Just before I left to come here."

We'd wandered around the corner to Newtown Lane. Into some clothing shop, the kind I never went into, filled with leather jackets, silk scarves and dresses, and CKone eau de toilette.

I let her remark about my showing her around go without comment. Let Nevada correct it. She'd only just arrived at Roundelay that morning.

I wanted to call Alex before he left for the theater. I looked at my watch (five P.M.) and she saw me do it.

"Do you have a date?"

"No. My mother might wonder where I am. I went down to the beach about noon, that's all."

"With that girl who threw rocks at you?"

"Yeah."

"Pffft! Is she your girlfriend?"

"No. Just a friend."

"Some friend."

Then she pulled this blue man's shirt off a hanger and held it up to me. It had yellow and white flowers stitched across the front.

She said, "This would fit you. No?"

"It would, but I wouldn't wear it."

"Sure you would. Wouldn't you?"

"No. . . . Don't buy me anything."

"You think I would buy this for you?"

"I don't know what you'd do."

"I don't even know you." She laughed. "I like you, but I don't go around buying shirts for someone I don't even know."

"I didn't think you *did*."

"You thought I was going to buy it for you. I know you did."

She was right about that.

I felt like an ass, but I shrugged and said, "You wouldn't be paying for it, anyway. Uncle Ben would."

"Do you like him, Lang?" She hailed a clerk, handed him the shirt and the Visa card.

"He's my mother's boss."

"So you don't."

"I don't know him."

"Do you like his music?"

"A lot."

She said to the clerk, "You can mail this for me?"

He said he could.

She wrote down an address while she talked to me. "What about Cali?"

"I don't know much about her. Do you?"

"There's a portrait of them together in the guest room. It's the only picture of her at Roundelay. It's a very formal pose, but the odd thing is she has a nose-bleed."

"Are you kidding?"

"No. . . . And I can't imagine Uncle Ben loving someone so passionately. He's so stern. . . . And that Franklin—he looks like something out of a wax museum."

She pushed the address across the counter, and the clerk said it would be extra to mail anything overseas.

"Okay!" she said brightly.

I figured the grape picker was going to have a new shirt. A $320 one. A Yohji Yamamoto.

TWELVE

"*What's* her name?" Alex asked.

"Huguette Haun. . . . That's why I didn't call sooner. Are you on your way out the door?"

"Almost. Huguette what?"

"Haun."

"*H-a-u-n?*"

"I guess."

"Huguette *Haun*?"

"Yes. What's the big deal?"

"Do you know who she is, Lang?"

"She's the daughter of a friend of Nevada's. She calls Nevada 'Uncle Ben.'"

"Lang, dear, she's Cali's *daughter*."

"I didn't even know she had a daughter."

"Cali married a man named Leonard Haun. They had one child. You just spent the afternoon with her."

"She's the one I told you about: the one Nevada wanted me to entertain this summer."

"My Gawd! And you refused."

"You said good for me last night."

"I didn't know it was Cali Coss's daughter!"

"What difference does it make?"

"Aren't you curious? What's she like?"

"I thought you were rushing out the door."

"I am. But what's she like?"

60

"I don't *believe* you."

"I don't believe *you*. Don't you have any curiosity?"

"I'm not starstruck, Alex."

"Okay. Skip it!"

"You can meet her this weekend."

"I *can*?"

"I guess you can."

"I wouldn't mind."

"Do you mean that?"

"Why don't we take her to a movie? I have to run, Lang. I love you."

"Love you too," I said, but I was teed off.

I hung up wondering how I was going to backtrack, how I was going to tell Nevada that both Alex and I would entertain her this weekend. I wondered if he'd agree to it . . . just this one time.

THIRTEEN

A Schwinn Tempo went with the caretaker's cottage. Mom was in a tizzy because she was nearly out of the homemade bread Nevada liked, and what if he wanted sandwiches for lunch that day?

I knew the farm where she got the bread, so I headed out around seven A.M. to get some for her.

The Range Rover was parked down by the gate. The rottweilers were diving into their food. Huguette was standing there in white shorts and a yellow T-shirt, watching with a frown on her face.

"Lang! Come here, please!"

"Are *you* feeding them now?"

"I'm trying to. That one won't eat, though."

"That's C. He always waits until the others are finished."

"So that's what he's up to? What does C stand for?"

I got off the bike. I told her Nevada's theory about not naming things you didn't want to get attached to.

"They're just guard dogs," I said. "Do you always get up this early?"

"This isn't early. I've already been to town."

"What's there to do in town at this hour?" Nothing much was open before nine.

"What do you care? First you think I'm going to buy you a shirt, and next you want to know all my business."

She was smiling, though; she seemed to have this game in her.

So I blurted out, "Next I wonder if you want to go to a movie Sunday night."

"Oh, you *do*? How come you do now? Uncle Ben said you might have other things to do than show me the sights."

"You could come with me and a friend."

"The rock thrower?"

"No. It's a male friend."

"What movie?"

"I don't know what's playing."

"So you just want my company?"

"Yes."

"How are we going to get there, on your bicycle?"

"It's your Uncle Ben's bicycle."

"Am I going to go there on the handlebars?"

"What does it matter how we go there?"

"Uncle Ben said maybe you were embarrassed because you don't have a car to take me in, and that's why you might not ask me places."

"Uncle Ben might not know we can walk from here to town."

"Or Franklin can take us."

"Or Franklin can take us."

"I accept," she said.

"What kind of movies do you like?"

"I don't like guns going off and people bleeding."

"Do you like comedies?"

"Some comedies. . . . Look! C's eating now."

I got back on my bike. "Then all is well. . . . When the local paper comes out tomorrow, it'll list the movies. You can pick the one we'll see."

"Where are you off to?" she asked.

"First you want to buy me a shirt, and next you want to know all my business," I said. "I'll call you tomorrow."

FOURTEEN

"I see you changed your mind, Lang."

"You mean about Huguette?"

I hadn't heard him coming. I was chopping wood, helping the groundsman clear away the old trees that had fallen down near the road. Nevada was paying me twenty dollars an hour.

"She said you're taking her to a movie Sunday."

I leaned on the axe and wiped my brow with the back of my hand. There was no sweat on him. He was all in black, per usual, a Gitane hanging from his lips.

"Yes. My friend's joining us."

"So she said. Does he live out here?"

I told him Alex's name, and that he was playing in *Hamlet*, so he would come out late Saturday night and go back Monday morning.

"How old is he?"

"Nineteen."

"Does he drink?"

"Neither of us drinks."

"You can take the Aurora. You might want to go someplace after for dinner."

"Thanks anyway, Mr. Nevada. We'd prefer to walk."

I didn't want to be indebted to him, or want him to think it was the beginning of "the deal" he'd set forth that Monday.

He reached into his pocket. "Since you're walking, you might want to eat at The Palm. It's down the street from the theaters. They're known for their steaks, and their lobsters." He pulled out a leather wallet.

I shook my head. "It'll be our treat," I said. "It won't be a regular thing. Just this once."

"That would be an expensive treat."

"I was thinking we could come back to the cottage after. I'd pick up some pizza. She might like to try our food."

"They have pizza all over France, even in the sticks," he said. "I think she'd enjoy going out." He took several hundred-dollar bills from his wallet. "Just this once."

He held out the money.

"No thanks. Maybe we'll pick up Chinese food."

"Or Lucy could make a light supper for you."

"My mother has Sundays off," I said.

He said, "I see. . . . You won't let anyone help you, is that it?"

"I figured she'd do what we do normally."

"The cottage is very small for the three of you and your mother."

"My mother has a date," I said. He looked as surprised as I'd felt when she told me about it. But she'd waved her hands as though she was shooing away a fly and mumbled something about not *that* kind of date. The only place she ever went was to the Presbyterian

Church on Main Street. I figured she'd met a friend there, maybe several people. Maybe she was going out with a group. I doubted that she'd be dating a man. Not so soon. She'd just said good-bye to one; she'd said she always found Mr. Not Quite Right, instead of Right himself.

Nevada said, "I have a dinner date too. I'm renewing old acquaintances to introduce to Huguette, so I appreciate this."

"It's just this one time, though."

"I heard you. . . . If you want to come back to Roundelay, you may. But please leave by eleven thirty."

Alex would be ecstatic. I couldn't refuse that offer.

"Thanks," I said. "We might." We would. I was sure of that.

I started to pick up the axe and he said, "One more thing, Lang."

"Sir?"

"I know what Huguette's up to." He pronounced her name the way she said you'd get nothing pronouncing it that way. "She took over the feeding of the rottweilers so she could leave the house early mornings. She goes into town. To call *him*, I suspect."

I thought of the $320 blue shirt.

"I don't know anything about it," I said.

He took a long drag from his cigarette and looked back toward Roundelay. "I can control things on this end. I have her passport. But if you should hear anything, or observe anything, I'd appreciate the information."

"I'll only be seeing her this one Sunday night," I said.

"I *heard* you," he said, "and you heard me."

FIFTEEN

After a lousy movie starring Al Pacino and a lot of guns, we hiked down the street to a place called Sam's for pizza. Nevada was right. They did have pizza all over France, even in the sticks. She said it was her favorite food.

"Either that," Alex said, "or she's giving us a break. Pizza's the only cheap thing in this town!"

She'd gone into the women's. We sat across from each other, grinning. Alex in the same blue blazer with the gold buttons he'd worn the first time I'd ever laid eyes on him in Barnes & Noble.

"I love you, Spartacus," I said softly. It was one of Tony Curtis's lines spoken to Kirk Douglas in an old movie. I'd say it to Alex times we were out somewhere together in public. I'd put my foot against his ankle under tables. My eyes would look all over his face. . . . Our secret games together.

Alex said, "I thought you said she didn't like movies with guns going off."

"Guns going off and people bleeding. She picked it."

"You knew Al Pacino was in it. That should have told you it wouldn't be a day at the beach."

She was back.

"Guns going off and people bleeding! *Merde!* What a movie!"

She sat beside Alex, facing me. "That is the thing I hate about America. You never can feel safe. You can be mugged, stabbed—anything."

Alex said, "Do you know the difference between stabbing a man and killing a hog?"

"No," she said.

"One is assaulting with intent to kill, and the other is killing with intent to salt."

"*You!*" Huguette said.

Actors need lines written for them. Alex needed a comedy routine, or he'd resort to riddles and puns. He wasn't a world-class wit, wasn't comfortable with small talk. Alex was the serious type. It was what I liked about him.

"What *about* me?" Alex said.

"You and your one-worders."

"One-liners," I corrected her.

As we'd walked to the movies, Huguette had told us that Nevada's French was so bad, she'd asked him to please speak English. Although French was her first language, she spoke English fluently, only occasionally stymied by certain expressions and slang, like *one-liner*, and like the one the day we'd gone shopping: *burrowed* a hole instead of *burned* a hole in her pocket.

We ordered pizza and Caesar salad, and as we ate it, Alex trotted out all his props for socializing. He analyzed her handwriting, a skill he'd picked up from an actor who posed as Dr. Scribe at parties, between jobs. And he did his astrology bit. He was a believer like a lot of actors: superstitious, fascinated by the occult. For my birthday he'd promised to have my horoscope done by this woman who the lead in *Hamlet* swore was prophetic.

Huguette was born under the sign of Scorpio, which Alex said was the sexiest sign of the Zodiac.

"A lot of good that does me here," she said. "You know the sign I'd like to be under?"

"What sign?" Alex said.

"The sign that says Aniane."

"Uh-oh. Homesick?"

"You both know why I'm here, don't you?"

I said, "Yes."

"So now we have the ice crusher."

"The icebreaker," I said.

"I can talk about him," she said.

I said, "Feel free."

SIXTEEN

Before we left Sam's, she showed us a black-and-white photograph of Martin Le Vec, who could have been Leonardo DiCaprio's double.

As we walked toward Roundelay, she told us that he had hair the color of the terra-cotta canal-tile roofs you saw all over la Moyenne Vallée de l'Hérault, and that his eyes were the color of dried lavender.

Alex would catch my eyes and roll his, wink and grin at the fun of hearing her go on (and on) about Martin. She pronounced it Mar*ten*.

He worked at a *mas*, a farm on the road between Aniane and Gignac.

"Picking grapes?" I said.

Her eyes flashed angrily. "He does *everything*! He is boss of the crew!"

He was seventeen, six foot three, "and talk about sexy!" she said.

"Talk about it," Alex teased.

"No! That I do *not* tell you!"

The rottweilers barked for emphasis.

The gates at Roundelay swung open. The lamps lighting the driveway turned on.

"How did that happen?" I said.

"Franklin sees us," she said. "And now that we're here, he can go. I told Uncle Ben we don't need a chaperone."

"I would say not," Alex said, "from all you've told us about your feelings for Martin."

"So now," she said as we went up the road toward Roundelay, "*you* tell me *your* feelings!"

Even though it was dark out, the soft yellow and pale-green colors in the huge living room seemed to wash it with this sunny glow.

While she put on some CDs with Alex's help, I counted three sofas, two settees, ten chairs, six benches, and four potted trees—all in that one room. It didn't look the least bit crowded.

On the far wall, near the marble fireplace, there was a portrait of Nevada, a shoulders-up view of him when he was younger, wearing a blue shirt the same color as his eyes. He looked like he'd stepped out of that old movie *Wuthering Heights*—Heathcliff fresh from the moors, dark and resentful.

Glass doors opened onto the terrace where I'd had lunch six days ago. I could hear the ocean in the distance.

The room was divided by a big round table covered with a yellow linen cloth and piled with books.

While an old Smashing Pumpkins album played, we began pawing through the books, mostly expensive, coffee-table art types.

One book had a photograph of the Leaning Tower of Pisa. Alex made some dim-witted crack about what made it lean was that it never got anything to eat.

"No more one-worders!" Huguette said. "I want to hear about you!"

"I believe in pheromones," said Alex.

"What are they?"

"They're why you love your Martin. We all give off these secretions that are irresistible to the one who responds to them."

I knew the play. It was called *You Made Me Love You*. Before Alex had landed the roles in *Hamlet*, he had tried out for the Scientist—a minor speaking part. This young genius discovers a way to produce the pheromone that will attract a beautiful girl to a rich sheik who wants to marry her.

"Love"—Alex never forgot anything he'd once memorized—"is what we name it, but it's pheromones that create this compelling chemistry between two people. It is what pulls you toward another like a nail sliding down to a magnet."

"Pheromones?" Huguette said. "I never heard of them!"

"One day," Alex said, "I was in a Barnes & Noble bookstore. The one on Twenty-second and Sixth."

I felt my stomach turn over.

Alex said, "I was there to hear this old Chet Baker album."

I tried to get his eye. He wouldn't look at me. We hadn't talked about it, but I'd thought he'd have the sense to shut up about us, since we were only seeing her this one night. What was the point?

My mother said once that coming out to strangers was a little like knocking over a wineglass at a dinner party. You stopped the flow of conversation instantly. There was the mop-up; the assurances it wasn't your fault, it could have happened to anybody—all the boring business of attending to all that.

Then Alex said, "And *she* was there to hear this new George Michael album."

"*She?*" said Huguette. "Who's she?"

"Lynn"—his father's name for me. "The love of my life."

I'd never heard Alex describe our first meeting. I didn't mind that I was in the third person with a sex change. As he talked, that moment went from the usual glib cover-up to something dizzy and sweet. I knew from his tone he felt it, too.

"So where is she?" Huguette asked at the end.

"She lives in New York."

Alex used to say that in that closet we all tried so hard to come out of were all the letters you wrote home changing *he* to *she*; all the memories of saying "Hi, there!" brightly to someone getting off a train you haven't seen in ages and want to hug to death; all the secret, long looks across the crowded room; all the times you didn't say who *you* were with last night while others *did* say; all the artifice, evasion, subterfuge, and hiding that goes into being gay.

Alex gave me that look that always made me feel my blood jump in my veins.

Then we heard a low buzzing hum, and Huguette looked at her watch. "Eleven fifteen. Is that Uncle Ben already?"

"He said we had until eleven thirty!"

"Come on," she said, and we followed her out into the hall, where a tiny screen monitored the action down by the gates.

"It's the Aurora," Huguette said, "so it's Franklin. But what's this? He has a girl with him."

I almost didn't recognize Franklin in a sport coat and pants, instead of the usual dark suit. But I recognized my mother. Franklin had gotten out of the sleek white car and gone around to help her from the passenger seat. He was about to walk her down the path to our cottage.

"He *does* have a girl with him!" Huguette said. "Where did *she* come from?"

"The same place I come from," I told her. "The caretaker's cottage."

"Your mother?" Alex said. "Is *he* her date?"

"It looks that way," I said. "We'd better go too."

"But I was just going to ask you about *yourself*, Lang."

"Another time," I said.

My mother was already in her room by the time we got down to the cottage.

There were two bedrooms in the place, mine and hers.

The couch in the small living room was made up with sheets, a cotton blanket, and a pillow. Same as the night before. Same as always when Alex came to visit. A silent reminder from my mother that no matter where we were for the summer, it was *her* home and we played by her rules.

Alex laughed. "Next week Nyack!"

"Nyack?"

"My parents' twentieth anniversary, remember? You promised you'd come with me."

Then he sat down and began taking off his shoes. "I like Huguette," he said, "but I wish she'd told us about Cali instead of Mar*ten*. Maybe next time."

"There won't be a next time," I said.

"How are you going to avoid her? She's going to be right up there for the rest of the summer."

"I just am," I said. "The masquerade is over, although I liked hearing your version of our first meeting."

"I meant everything I said, Lynn." He chuckled and held out his arms.

Later, the shock of seeing my mother with Franklin gave me insomnia. I didn't even know if Franklin was his first name or his last. I only knew he reminded me of one of these snooty salesmen in a high-class men's store, or a mortician. I couldn't remember him ever smiling.

I was still awake when I heard the rottweilers announce Nevada's return.

SEVENTEEN

I waited until Monday afternoon, when Alex was on the jitney headed into New York.

Then I said, "Since when do you date Franklin?"

"Since last night. We only went to dinner—a very *late* dinner thanks to you, Alex, and Huguette."

"*Eu*gette," I said. "If you say her name *You*gette, you get nothing."

"We had to wait until you got back to Roundelay."

"Why didn't you just say you were going out with him?"

"Look at your face. The answer's right there."

"Well, I'm not overjoyed, you're right. For God's sake, Mom, he moves like a robot."

"He's a little wooden, that's true, but he's pleasant."

"It's a little hard to take, you with Franklin."

"Oh, and you with Alex is easy to take."

She had me there. I grumped around for a while as she reminded me that she was only thirty-seven, not quite dead yet, not a nun who'd taken vows of celibacy, and not averse to having a life beyond our life together.

We were in the middle of this discussion when a knock came at the door.

Huguette was standing there in these tight gray sweats that rode low on her hips, and a white half shirt that showed she'd been sunbathing at some point when she didn't have on that outfit. There was a wide gap of white skin above her waist.

"Can you do me a favor?" she said.

"What's that?"

"Drive me into the village?"

I opened the screen door, but she shook her head and said, "I'm not coming in. You come out."

I walked through the door and we stood in the small yard, a few feet away from the field with the dandelions and the snakes.

"How long will this take?" I asked. "I don't mean just this one time, either."

"Uncle Ben says he doesn't like me out driving around alone. Besides, he's not sure my French license is good in the United States."

"I was going to tell you the other night, but I forgot. He's wise to the reason you take the Range Rover out early mornings."

"I know. He's forbidden me to do it. He says he wants me to have someone with me who can also drive."

"There's always Franklin."

"Not Franklin! He's Uncle Ben's spy."

I could see the white Aurora parked down by the gates.

"I suppose I'm supposed to sit in the car and cool my heels while you call Mar*ten* in France."

"Do you have something against pheromones?" She dangled the car keys at me.

From the doorway, my mother called out, "Go ahead, Lang! Hello, Huguette. I'm Lang's mother."

I liked Huguette for saying, "Hello, *Mrs*. Penner." (Nevada always referred to her as Lucy.) "Wouldn't it be a big help to you, too, if he had the use of a car?"

Like a lot of people who live their lives in New York, my mother didn't drive.

"A *big*, big help!" my mother agreed.

"It doesn't mean I'm going to become your personal chauffeur," I grumbled at Huguette.

She said, "What makes you think I'd want you for my personal chauffeur? You've got such a big face!"

"A big *head*!" I said, following her down toward the Aurora.

EIGHTEEN

"I never knew Cali," she said. "Phoenix Haun is my legal name. The Roshans always call me Huguette. They're my family, just as Aniane is my home."

It was her idea to take a picnic lunch days I went driving with her. We'd stop somewhere and she'd put a blanket down, and a blue-and-white-checked cloth on the ground. We'd feast on cheese and pâté and fruit: her choices. I would have packed tunafish sandwiches and Oreos.

"Uncle Ben tells me that Cali was the love of his life, but she was only with him four years. That's so sad."

That day we were down by the Nature Preserve, where there were ducks that would have chosen sandwich scraps over pâté too.

They padded around us as we sat there talking. There were more in the stream near us; there were all sorts of colored birds in the trees above us. People strolled by feeding the ducks, pointing at the birds, studying them with binoculars.

I don't remember how she started on the subject of Cali. I know I didn't bring it up. We didn't probe; we didn't ask leading questions. That was what I liked about our times together . . . that, and something else I'd noticed a few times when I was someplace with

Brittany. There was not the self-conscious feeling I some-times had when Alex and I went places together. Put a boy and a girl on a blanket in the sun and the whole world smiled at you. Put two fags there and the smiles turned crooked, the eyebrows raised, you held your breath waiting for the wisecracks.

"Tell me something," I said. "Why did your mother always say 'Pain over' when she sang? Do you know?"

"Call her Cali, not my mother. My aunt is my mother," Huguette said. "It wasn't 'pain over.' Cali said, 'Paint over it.' It's from a song Uncle Ben wrote. It was Cali's favorite of all his songs. Mother said Uncle Ben never liked it, never released it."

"What does it mean?"

"The real title is 'How to Refurbish a Chair or a Broken Heart.' Someday I'll play it for you. Uncle Ben has it at Roundelay. . . . It isn't about Cali, either."

"What is it about?"

"It's about continuing, putting the past behind you. It's about his childhood: the death of his mother when he was very young. . . . He wrote it for his father."

"The accompanist."

"Yes. Armand Nevada was an accompanist. But he was a brilliant musician. A classical musician. He was educated, not like Uncle Ben, who pores over Bartlett's quotations so he can pretend he's well read. 'Paint Over It' was the first song Uncle Ben ever wrote for his father, but the old man hated it. He called it 'sentimental rock slop.' My mother said it nearly killed Uncle Ben."

"He got even with 'Dad's Advice.'"

"Yes. With nearly every song after that, too."

"The old man never approved of Nevada, hmm?"

"It must have been hard to approve of Uncle Ben back then. Or Cali. They were always on drugs. I have her diary in Aniane. Part of my inheritance." She let out a scornful laugh. "She'd write things like 'Smoked bowls and did acid.' That would be one day's entry. She finally ended up in a place called Hazeldon, for rehab."

"A lot of them did."

"Uncle Ben and Cali got success too soon. I don't think much of success, do you?"

"I haven't had a taste of it."

"I haven't either. I don't have any wish for it. It brings you unhappiness. Martin says happiness is a vineyard, good weather, and enough help to get the job done."

"Where do you come in?"

"I share it with him, no?"

"So you'd settle for a life in Aniane?"

"Settle? You should see Aniane. You should see Martin. *Cali* settled when she got rescued by Leonard Haun. Mother says there was no way Cali could have loved a pint-sized insurance executive with an ulcer, whose idea of a good time was a round of bridge. My biological father! Cali was desperate for security!"

She looked at her watch suddenly. "*Mon dieu!* Look at the time, Lang! I said I'd be back by four to play tennis with Uncle Ben!"

That week, our lunches got later and later as we lingered talking.

Alex complained that I saw more of her than I did of him. Sometimes I would get back to the cottage too late to call him before he left for the theater. That had never happened until she came into my life.

Nevada was waiting for us when we arrived at Roundelay. He was sitting in the old Ford down by the gates as we pulled in.

He called out his car window, "I was going to look for you except I didn't know where to look! It's five o'clock, Huguette! I was worried about you!"

"You know I'm with Lang," she answered. "No need to worry."

"Drive on," he told her. "I want a word with Lang."

She said she'd see me the next day at ten A.M. I had a jitney reservation for six P.M. It was the weekend I'd go up to Nyack with Alex.

I got out of the Aurora and she went up the drive.

The rottweilers never barked when Nevada was on the scene.

I walked over to the Ford, around to the driver's side.

"Do you feel okay about driving Huguette?" he asked.

"I have the hang of it," I said. "She's good company, too."

"Has she got the hang of leaving Roundelay without stopping somewhere to phone this Le Vec?"

"She hasn't made any calls that I know about." It was true. But it had been only one week. He didn't ask me if she had made any purchases—like a man's leather Gucci wallet and a Whitney Houston CD. ("Does Martin speak English?" I'd asked her when she bought it. She'd said that he knew the English in songs.)

Nevada said, "The Fourth of July they're having a big celebration out in Montauk. Fireworks, rock bands, a surprise appearance by Cog Wheeler, that sort of thing. Do you know The Failures?"

"Who doesn't? They're opening at Sob Story the next day."

"Huguette has never seen an American Fourth of July. I think she'd like to go."

"Are you going to take her?" I knew he was angling for me to go along.

"I can't go to those affairs. My presence in the audience spoils it for everyone else."

I knew what he meant. That first weekend when Alex and I went to a movie, we saw Billy Joel get mobbed while he was in the ticket line with his daughter—and they were used to seeing Billy Joel in that town. I could imagine what would happen if Nevada showed up anywhere.

I said, "My birthday is Saturday night, the third. Alex will arrive late that night and stay till Monday."

"I could get three tickets," he said.

"We've made plans, Mr. Nevada." We hadn't. But

neither of us liked those grungy Seattle bands, and a threesy wasn't what we had in mind for my birthday celebration.

Nevada lit a Gitane, then said, "You'd have the use of the Aurora, of course. I'd reimburse you for any expenses the three of you incurred. It's a hot ticket, Lang."

"I thought I told you—"

He cut me off. "You told me. But you seem to enjoy her."

"I do enjoy her. It isn't *that*."

"Have you told her about yourself, Lang?"

"No."

"Why should you?" He sounded like my mother.

"Why shouldn't I?" I shot back.

"Lang, Lang, listen to me: Someone once wrote 'Every truth has two sides; it is well to look at both, before we commit ourselves to either.'"

I figured he'd dug that one out of *Bartlett's*.

I said, "Someone else once wrote: 'If my lies you believe, then I might let you breathe.'"

He squeezed his eyes shut for a second, then opened them and growled, "I wasn't much older than you are when I wrote that. You're a pain in the ass, Penner!"

He took off in the old Ford, heading through the gates of Roundelay.

That was when he first started calling me by my last name.

NINETEEN

"Alex! Over here!"

"Here's Alex!"

"Hello, Alex!"

There were around thirty guests at the twentieth-anniversary party for Alex's parents.

We rode up to Nyack with an aunt of Alex's who was meeting her husband there.

There was a gingerbread house overlooking the Hudson River, high on a hill, with a yard filled with Alex's family.

I remember a Robert Frost poem I memorized in eighth grade: the one about two roads diverging in a woods, and someone taking the one less traveled by.

It was a little borrowed glory to help me through dark days when I was beginning to accept what I was.

That Sunday everyone seemed to have taken the road *most* traveled by. Alex and I were the odd couple. No room in the ark for the likes of us.

Peter, Alex's twin, clapped his arm around his shoulder and called out, "Uncle Henry? Get a shot of me and Alex!"

A man pointed a camera at them as I stepped aside.

Then Peter pushed a redheaded girl in between Alex and himself, saying: "Uncle Henry?"

Uncle Henry obliged.

Peter said, "Alex, this is my girlfriend, Tina Lopez."

"How do you do, Tina? This is my friend, Lang Penner. Peter? You remember Lang."

"Hi." Peter never said my name, nor met my eyes when he greeted me.

"Hello, Peter and Tina," I said.

Tina had a camera too.

Tina said, "Alex and Peter? Hold still!"

Uncle Henry said, "Tina? Will you take a picture of me with Alex and Peter?" He handed Tina his camera.

Peter said, "Tina? Let Lang take the picture, and then you can get in here."

I took the camera from Tina. I took the picture.

"Alex!" a woman called. "Come and see your cousin. You haven't seen Timmy since he started walking!"

I wandered around by myself for a while. I went into the house to use the bathroom, which was adorned with photographs of Alex and Peter and Mr. and Mrs. Southgate, in all sorts of poses, in all seasons, at all ages.

I looked at the books in the shelves lining the walls, and I flipped through a copy of *Time* magazine. I petted the cat asleep on the couch and watched the party from the window for a while.

Then I went out in the yard to the grill, where Alex's father was outfitted in cook's regalia, complete with a tall, white, mushroom-shaped chef's hat.

He was an older, heavier version of Alex, basting

ribs and wiping his forehead with the back of his hand.

"I thought you were in the Hamptons, Lynn?"

I never bothered correcting him anymore.

"I am, but not *all* the time."

"So I see. Well, make yourself useful. Pass that tray of ribs around."

I went from couple to couple until I came to Alex's mother, settled into a sling chair with a martini. She was a good-looking woman with black curly hair, feeling no pain. "Hello, Lang. I thought you were in the Hamptons this summer?"

"I am, but not *all* the time. Congratulations on your anniversary!"

"Thank you, dear. How's your mother?"

"She's fine, thank you."

"Alex says she's working for Ben Nevada. That couldn't be easy, but what's easy?"

"*This* is," a woman seated beside her said, and she raised her glass to Mrs. Southgate and took a sip of her martini.

She said, "Who's this?"—looking at me.

"Lang Penner," said Mrs. Southgate.

"Penner?" said the woman. "Who married a Penner?"

"He's a friend of Alex's," said Mrs. Southgate.

"Are you an actor?" the woman asked.

"He's not anything," said Mrs. Southgate. "He's still

in high school. You're still in high school, aren't you, Lang?"

"Yes, ma'am."

"From New York?" the woman asked.

"Yes, ma'am."

"Alex is a wonderful actor!" the woman said.

"Yes, he is," I said.

"Peter's here with his girlfriend," said Mrs. Southgate. "Her father is a big film director: José Lopez."

"Do you know Peter?" the woman asked me.

"Yes, I know him."

"José Lopez has something to do with that new sitcom *Sun Fun*," said Mrs. Southgate.

The woman said, "I never watch sitcoms."

"I don't either," I said.

"I'm *Dorothy* Southgate," the woman said as she stood up. "I'm Alex's aunt."

"Didn't I introduce you?" Mrs. Southgate said. "I thought I introduced you."

"I have to find my daughter," said Dorothy Southgate.

"Did she bring the baby?" Mrs. Southgate asked.

"The baby's with a sitter today," said Dorothy Southgate.

Mrs. Southgate watched her leave.

She said, "Thank God I've got Peter! If I thought I'd have to go through life without grandchildren, I'd throw in the proverbial towel. You're an only child, aren't you, Lang?"

"Yes. There's just me."

"How does your mother feel about it?"

"How does she feel about what?"

"How does she feel about not ever having grand-children?"

"We haven't discussed it, Mrs. Southgate."

"If you ever get around to discussing it," she said, "take plenty of Kleenex along—she'll appreciate it." She took a big sip of her martini. None of the guests were hurrying our way. Alex often said that his mother, in her cups, could frighten ravenous bees away from honey.

Mrs. Southgate rested her martini on her knee. She waved one hand in a circle. "This is what it's all about, Lang. Anniversaries, grandkids, family gatherings." And from behind me I heard Alex add, "And Stolichnaya, Mom, with a whisper of vermouth."

"It's about that, too," she said. "Find me a cigarette somewhere, honey. I never should have given up smoking entirely. There's such a thing as being too pure, not that it'd be anything *you* have to worry about."

"We'll be right back," said Alex.

We walked in the opposite direction, away from the party, down along the path, where there was a good view of the Hudson River from the cliff.

"How are you holding up?" he asked me.

"I'm hanging in there."

"I don't want to stay much longer. There's a cousin

of mine heading back to New York; he said he'd take us in."

"It's a shame to leave when we're having so much fun," I said.

"Ha ha," he said.

"Why do you *do* this, Alex? Why do I have to come to these things with you?"

"Peter brings *his* dates."

"What happens when Peter has children? Do we rescue some poor orphans from China?"

He wasn't listening to me. He said, "I was basting more ribs for Dad, and he seized that opportunity to give me a lecture about AIDS. He said, 'I mention this because I read somewhere that you people are going back to being promiscuous.' I said, 'This is the sixth time you've met Lang. Peter hasn't shown up at these things with the same girl twice. Tell Peter about safe sex, not me.'

"So he said, 'Why do you always compare yourself to Peter? The only way you're like Peter is your looks!' And I said, 'I'm a lot prettier than Peter, wouldn't you say?' '*Pretty*'s the word, all right, Alex,' he said, 'and look where being pretty has gotten you!'"

"Why *do* you always compare yourself with Peter?" I said.

"Because he's my gawdamned twin!"

We stood there looking out at the long, low-hung Tappan Zee Bridge in the distance.

92

I told him about Nevada's offer to get us tickets for the Fourth of July celebration.

"I've never understood one word Cog Wheeler sings!"

"I didn't think you wanted to go."

"It's your birthday weekend, love. We'll do what *you* want."

"I don't want to go either."

"You sure?"

"That isn't how I want to spend my birthday."

"I never know with you anymore."

"You never know with *me* anymore?"

"I don't."

"What are you talking about?"

"Your girlfriend. You spend all that time with her."

"Not that much," I lied.

"Do you know what she did? She wrote me a note thanking me for last Sunday."

"She said she was going to."

"She sent it to the theater."

"I told her to, since you say your mail's always being swiped from your box."

"It was waiting backstage last night."

"So? What about it?"

"She closed saying she was going to get some 'sleep that knits up the ravell'd sleave of care,' and then she added, 'as they say in *Macbeth*!' . . . Migawd!" He hit his forehead with his palm.

I said, "Give her a break. She was just trying to impress you by quoting Shakespeare."

"She impressed me all right!" said Alex. "She named the play!"

"What *about* it?"

"She named it, Lang. In a letter to the theater!"

It took me a second or so to remember.

It's bad luck to refer to that play by name. Actors really believe it is. It's part of stage lore, the same as you're never supposed to wish an actor good luck; you say something like "Break a leg" instead.

Alex took all that very seriously.

I said, "You mean you can't even *write* the name?"

"If you *have* to write it, you write 'the Scottish play.'"

"How would she know that?"

"The actor playing Horatio flubbed his lines last night! Cal Gherin *never* makes mistakes! And I got indigestion in the first act!"

"Come on, Alex. Get a life!"

"There's something unlucky about her."

"Last week you said you liked her."

"Last week *you* said the masquerade was over. Did you tell her about us?"

"Not yet."

"I didn't think so."

"I will."

"I won't hold my breath."

He turned and walked away from me. I knew it wasn't just Huguette who had him so steamed. It was the way his family treated us. He was always in a lousy mood after one of the Southgate conclaves.

Before we left, everyone lined up on the lawn for a family photograph.

"Would you mind, Lynn?" Mr. Southgate handed me his camera.

"Tina?" Peter called out. "C'mon! I want you in this!"

"Make sure you get everyone in!" Mr. Southgate called to me as I focused on all of them.

Dorothy Southgate said, "I can take one with Lang in it, after he takes this one."

"Lynn doesn't want to be in it," Mr. Southgate said.

"Lang!" Alex snapped. "Lang, Dad! For Gawd's sake get it right for once!"

Mr. Southgate muttered, *"You* get it right, why don't you?"

"Say cheese!" I said.

"Brie!" Mrs. Southgate laughed.

That got them all going.

"Roquefort!" someone shouted.

"Camembert!" Peter called out.

"Gorgonzola!" from Tina.

"Port-Salut!" Mr. Southgate.

Alex and I squeezed into the rear seat of a green Geo for the ride back to New York.

We weren't talking.

I was thinking of all the family pictures everywhere in the house. Then I thought of Huguette telling me about that portrait of Nevada in her bedroom, and Cali with a nosebleed. She'd told me that she'd finally asked Nevada about it, asked him what it meant.

He'd said that it was some whim of the artist's, that when he first saw it, he was furious. But Cali liked it. Cali made Nevada keep it. She'd said it was "honest." Shortly after it was painted, she'd left Nevada.

I'd asked Huguette what she thought it meant.

"How do *I* know?" she'd said. "Maybe the artist saw her distress. . . . The funny thing is that's the one picture where I look like her. I resented it being there where I can see it every morning when I wake up. But now I don't. She looks so beautiful and vulnerable."

"Well, she's got a nosebleed. Who wouldn't look vulnerable?"

"I think I remind him of her, a lot. I think Uncle Ben imagines I'm in distress, and that maybe he can save me when he couldn't save her. He'll save me from Martin, he thinks. Some screwbat idea like that!"

"Screwball," I'd said.

I wanted to tell Alex about it, but I was already beginning to try to keep Huguette out of our conversations. I knew Alex was jealous of her, and of all that I was getting involved in at Roundelay.

When we saw the lights of the George Washington Bridge, Alex did his imitation of Clark Gable, the last line from *The Misfits*, when he told Marilyn Monroe, "Just head for that big star straight on. The highway's under it, and it'll take us right home."

He reached for my hand.

From the front seat his cousin said, "Humphrey Bogart, right?"

TWENTY

"Happy Birthday!" my mother said. "Nick Ball called to say he's at Allie's in Sag Harbor. He wants you to call him."

I was fresh from the shower. Huguette was waiting for me in the Aurora, down by the gates. It was pouring out. We were going to a one-o'clock matinee, something with Julia Roberts in it.

"Are you going out with Franklin tonight?"

"Yes. We're going to see the new show at Guild Hall. Then we're having dinner somewhere. When is Alex arriving?"

"Very late," I said. "There's a cast meeting after the performance. He has a ride."

"Then he's going to wake up the rottweilers."

"Probably. Sorry about that."

"I wish you could get hold of him and tell him to get dropped off down the road by the short cut. Then he could come up that back path without the dogs barking."

"I'll try. Mom, what's going on with you and Franklin?"

"I like him. You would, too, if you'd give him a chance."

"A chance to what? Be my daddy?"

"He couldn't be any worse than the real one."

I blew her a kiss, grabbed an umbrella, and hurried out the door.

As I walked through the rain, I thought about Nick. He'd called about a week ago, as I was hurrying to get to Sob Story. He'd said he wanted to talk with me. Nevada was having people for dinner that night and Mom was helping Franklin load up the Range Rover with stew and salad. I'd told Nick I'd call him when I had more time.

We never saw Nevada's guests. Huguette said they were mostly musicians: people from his past. The Matero twins, who used to play backup, Twist—people like that.

Evenings, Huguette hung out with whoever was visiting Roundelay, or she holed up in her room writing long letters to Martin.

Most days I had odd jobs to perform around the estate. There was always something to do, and I'd need money in the fall when I went back to school. I was only getting six dollars an hour at Sob Story, working from five to ten P.M.

But some days Huguette and I played tennis, saw a movie, or drove around Southampton, Sag Harbor, Montauk: sightseeing.

I didn't tell Alex how much time we were spending together. I knew he'd nag at me again to tell her about us. I would when I found the right moment. I couldn't see just blurting it as I had that day with Brittany.

I wondered if that was what Nick wanted to talk

about. I'd never called him back because I had an idea it was. I dreaded discussing it with Nick. Alex always said if you can lose a friend by coming out to him, you aren't losing a friend. But it wasn't that easy. I'd known Nick all my life. I didn't want to test him that way. I was afraid of some big scene we'd never be able to get past.

That afternoon, the first words out of Huguette's mouth were "I have to call Martin before four o'clock. It'll be ten at night his time. His family goes to bed early, and I don't want to wake them up."

"There's a phone booth right across from the movies," I said. "We'll head over there as soon as we get out."

"Uncle Ben is having lunch at his agent's. Then he'll pick me up at four in front of Polo. I'll leave the car in the lot behind Polo, unless Alex wants to drive it to Roundelay when he gets here."

"He's got a ride," I said.

She never pushed on weekends, never asked what Alex and I were doing. I wouldn't, either, if I could hang out with Nevada's circle. I'd watch the cars head up past the gates: a Porsche, a Lexus, a SAAB, a Mercedes. I'd hear the music, sometimes live. That afternoon, after our matinee, Nevada was taking her to a small cocktail party at Mick Jagger's place in Montauk. Nevada never attended big parties. He rarely went to parties at all, rarely left Roundelay. But he was making exceptions that summer because of Huguette.

By then I was used to people turning to stare at her. She said it was her clothes. She said she'd never looked so good until she'd had Uncle Ben's Visa card. She used it to shop, have facials, manicures, have her hair styled.

That afternoon she had on a white T-shirt with a pink vest and pink satin jeans and black high-heeled sling-back shoes. I liked the way she dressed, but it was something more that made her stand out. An attitude, a sophistication—I didn't know the name for it. But even as we sat in the theater waiting for the movie to start, I noticed this grungy-looking guy, with a Red Dog beer cap tugged down to his eyebrows, staring at her. He was wearing a pair of those mirror glasses, the kind you look at and see yourself in. He'd look away when I'd see him watching her, then he'd look back.

I nudged her. "You've got a fan."

"Or else he's one of those series murderers."

"*Serial* murderers," I said. "He could be both, couldn't he?"

"With my luck, yes."

She kept looking at her watch all through the movie.

I whispered, "Don't worry. I checked. We'll be out at three twenty."

It didn't stop her.

She smelled like a fashion magazine. She'd told me she wore Joop. I'd asked my mother if she ever wore Joop, and she said who can afford Joop?

When we came out of the theater, she almost got run over by an Infiniti crossing the street. I caught up with her on the other side, in front of Polo, around the corner from the public pay phone.

The rain had stopped.

I said I was going down to The Grill and call backstage, leave Alex a message telling him not to be dropped off in front of the gates at Roundelay.

"Maybe we'll have time for a coffee together," Huguette said. "Uncle Ben is always late, and Martin never talks for very long when the whole family is right there. Let's try to do it, Lang."

Alex was between acts.

"You're not going to like this," he began, "and I have to talk fast, so don't blow your top, love."

Hamlet was closing that night. They'd all been given notice as they'd arrived for the matinee.

Before I could tell him I was sorry, he said, "There's a production of *Bus Stop* up on the Cape. The lead crashed his car into a tree last night. I've got a chance to replace him, Lang. This could be a big deal for me. I'm going up there."

"When?"

"Tomorrow morning. I'm sorry. I have to go."

"Tomorrow?"

"How do you think *I* feel? I wanted to be there for your birthday! You know that."

"What lousy luck!"

102

"You can blame your girlfriend, sweetheart. The Scottish play! Remember? You can tell her she closed us. Now she can have you all to herself." He laughed bitterly.

"So when will I see you?"

"Don't *whine*!" he said. "It isn't my fault! I'll call you tonight! I love you!"

He hung up.

I stood in front of Polo stewing. I was disappointed, but I was pissed, too! Pissed at the crack about Huguette having me all to herself, and pissed at him telling me not to whine. I knew sometimes I whined. I didn't need Alex to remind me. I didn't need to spend my birthday alone, either.

I had to keep my eye out for Nevada, warn her if he came early. He still asked me if she ever made phone calls when I was off places with her, and if she talked much about Martin. I'd lie. I seemed to be spending my summer lying: to Nevada about that, to Alex about how much time we spent together, and to Huguette about Alex and me being just buddies.

I stared at Polo's window display. They put every-thing but the kitchen sink in those windows. There were surfboards, real sand, seashells, striped awning chairs, dummies dressed in expensive clothes sitting on towels holding playing cards.

I waited . . . and I waited.

Then Huguette came around the corner all smiles.

She said, "I'm sorry it took so long. Now you're mad."

"No, I'm not."

"Just say you are. You'll feel better."

"But I'm not."

"You should see your face."

"It hasn't got anything to do with you."

"You always deny, Lang. That first day you thought I was going to buy you a shirt, you did the same thing. You said that you didn't think that, but you really did."

"The shirt again!"

"Do you want me to buy you a shirt? I'll buy you one for your birthday."

"For my birthday, just *forget* the shirt! Don't ever bring up the shirt again!"

"Maybe I want to give you something, though."

"Don't. I'd only give it back to you because I'm so mad!"

She laughed and punched my arm.

I wasn't going to tell her that Alex had to go up to the Cape, but suddenly I did.

"Oh, no! Oh, Lang! You'll be alone on your birthday!"

"I don't care about that!"

It began to rain again.

"I hate to leave you," she said. "Maybe you could come with us."

"I'm going to work," I said.

"On your birthday?"

"Who cares about my birthday? A birthday's just another day, for Gawd's sake!"

The Range Rover pulled into a handicapped parking

space, Nevada behind the wheel, the three chows with their heads out the window, their black tongues hanging down.

"Oh, he's right on the knob," Huguette said.

"Right on the *button*," I said. "Have a good time."

She took my hand and pressed a small package into it. "I didn't forget," she said. "Happy Birthday."

She gave me a quick kiss and a wave and ran off, trying to keep her slingbacks on her feet, the rain splashing her.

I stood in the doorway of Polo opening the present, lightning flashing suddenly in the sky.

It was in a tiny blue Tiffany box.

I remembered the day Brittany and I went to the beach in her mother's BMW. We'd talked about Deep Blue Something's hit "Breakfast at Tiffany's." That was the day I met Huguette . . . and I remembered when I first saw her I thought she looked like the actress in that film: Audrey Hepburn.

All of that seemed longer ago than just a few weeks.

I took out a small gold key chain, with a solid gold circle attached, something engraved in its center.

Paint Over It.

There was a card enclosed.

I will play it for you soon. But this will help you remember the summer, and it is good advice, anyway, even if it is not a perfect song. H.

TWENTY-ONE

Kevin McCaffery owned Sob Story. He drove a beige SAAB convertible with a license plate that said SAB STORY. Except for the "sizzling" steaks, all the dinners were brought in from a food concession, preprepared, frozen. But every day McCaffery took great pains to compose a "Daily Specials" menu:

- *Homemade Pot Roast fresh from the oven with Tiny Carrots, Onions, and Long Island Potatoes*
- *Our Chef's delicious Fillet of Boneless Chicken Breasts Sautéed with Lemon and Butter.*

Et cetera, et cetera.

In the kitchen I arranged the food on plates, pulled salads from plastic bags and doused them with dressing, cut pieces of cake and slices of pie, and scooped ice cream.

We were packed that weekend; we always were on the long weekends.

That was why I was surprised when McCaffery appeared in the kitchen at nine o'clock to tell me I was finished for the night.

"Take off your apron and get ready to leave."

"Is something wrong, sir?"

"Something's right for a change. Ben Nevada just called to say he wants to give a private party here tomorrow night in honor of The Failures."

"Since when are we open on Sundays?"

"Since he called. I'm going to Roundelay with you now, to discuss the details with him. C'mon, Lang. You've been moving in slow motion all night. What's with you?"

I hadn't been able to get my mind off Huguette and the gift she'd given me. It was so totally unexpected.

As we drove through the rain, McCaffery told me they'd done 120 dinners the night before and close to that already tonight. He said he supposed he had me to thank for the party Nevada was planning, and I told him honestly that it was the first I'd heard about it. I didn't even know Nevada had any connection with The Failures.

The only thing I *did* know Huguette had mentioned: that same article Nevada had told me he'd read in *Rolling Stone* about Cog Wheeler. Cog Wheeler had said that his song "Pop's Rap" was a tribute to Nevada, inspired by "Dad's Advice." Wheeler told the interviewer that Nevada's father sounded a lot like his own, and that he'd named his group The Failures because his father had once remarked that he was a failure and so were all his friends.

I'd never heard "Pop's Rap."

The only song of Cog Wheeler's that I really knew was his big hit "Heard About You."

Every time you turned on a radio that summer, you heard that fragile, reedy voice singing:

Heard about you,
Heard you couldn't be true,
Heard you did it with Sue,
Heard about you,
We've all heard about you.

It was about a guy whose girlfriend had ditched him for another girl. When Alex had heard it, he'd said he doubted there'd be a hit song about a girl losing her boyfriend to another boy. The public wouldn't go for that.

When we got to the gates at Roundelay, I said, "Let me off here."

The rottweilers were in good form, and McCaffery had to shout above them to be heard. "You come up to Roundelay with me, Lang."

"He's not expecting me."

"Just introduce me, okay?"

"He won't like it, Mr. McCaffery."

"Just introduce me and then leave!"

He didn't wait for any more protests from me. The gates opened and we went through them.

There were about a dozen cars parked outside.

I said, "I'm not going in."

"You work for me from five to ten," McCaffery said. "It's only nine twenty now."

He pulled in behind a Lexus, and we ran through the rain to the side door.

Nevada was right there waiting.

"Hello, Penner."

I said, "Mr. Nevada, this is Kevin McCaffery."

"I know who he is," he growled. "Hang your coats here on the rack."

"I'm not staying, sir," I said.

"Yes you are, Penner," he said.

McCaffery hung up his raincoat, and I put my jacket next to it.

"Come along," said Nevada.

I wondered why he'd given Franklin the night off when he was entertaining.

After we walked down the long hall, up two steps, down another hall, and into the living room, I knew why.

"Happy Birthday!" everyone shouted.

I just stood there.

While everyone sang, I looked around that huge yellow-and-green room with the three sofas, two settees, ten chairs, six benches, and four potted trees.

Some of the guests I knew. My mother and Franklin. Nick Ball and Allie Perez. And Huguette, of course, all smiles, hugging herself and laughing hard.

I didn't know the guy next to her, but I'd seen him before. He wasn't wearing the Red Dog beer cap, but he still had on the mirrored glasses.

When they'd finished singing "Happy Birthday," Huguette took him by the hand and brought him across to me.

"You remember the serial murderer," she said. "Lang, this is Cog Wheeler."

TWENTY-TWO

The Failures were there in full force, young girls with long hair, long legs, and short skirts following after them. Except for Cog Wheeler, the band had that grungy Seattle look.

He didn't. With his cap off there was the trademark shock of fire-red, spiky hair. But he wore no jewelry, only a watch. He had on a khaki T-shirt, black jeans, and black high-top sneakers. Despite a minor case of neck acne he looked clean and wholesome. I couldn't see his eyes, only my own staring back from the lenses of his dark glasses. He was skinny and taller than I was. After we were introduced, he led Huguette away.

"Heard About You" was blaring from the speakers.

I went over to my mother, who seemed uncomfortable sitting on one of the settees beside Franklin. I leaned down and gave her a kiss and whispered, "Whose idea was this?"

"Not mine, honey. Huguette planned this at the last minute, after she heard Alex couldn't come out. All I did was give her Nick's number."

I don't think Franklin had ever sat down in that room. He looked uncomfortable, too.

He got up and disappeared for a while, then returned wheeling in a cart with a huge cake on it.

There was another round of "Happy Birthday," and

before I cut the cake, Allie Perez said, "Make a wish!"

"I wish we all get our wishes this summer," I said.

"Now we won't," Nick said, laughing, "because you told your wish."

I cut the cake, and my mother helped Franklin pass it around on plates.

While Cog Wheeler was getting two plates for Huguette and himself, I went over to her.

"I want to talk to you," I said.

"Talk to me." She smiled.

"Somewhere we can be alone for a second."

"Come on," she said.

She took my hand and we walked through the living room to the hall. She had on this very sheer, short black dress and violet kickers with a silver ankle bracelet strapped to the left one.

"Thanks for this," I said, "and thanks for the key ring."

"That will remind you of all our picnics."

"Or it'll remind me that I don't have a car."

"You can take the Aurora anytime."

"I don't want to drive his car."

"Why do you resist Uncle Ben so, Lang? He likes you. He calls you Penner."

"I know." I could smell Joop.

I could see Cog Wheeler watching us from the living room. I said, "I think I was right. You do have a fan."

She looked over her shoulder at him. "He's very talented, isn't he?"

"Is he? I wouldn't know."

"Of course he is, Lang! He writes those songs."

"You can't hear the words when he sings them."

"You can if you listen hard."

I imitated him. "'eard bout ew, 'eard youcoulden ee ew.'"

She laughed and tugged at my shirt. "You don't want me to like him? Is that it?"

I thought, That *is* it, isn't it?

I said, "What about Mar*ten*?"

"Oh, you're worried about Martin, hmmm?"

"What about him?" I said.

"You're not worried about that. You just think nobody here can be with me but *you*."

"Is *that* it?" I said. I poked her arm with my finger. I could see her small breasts through her dress.

It was one of those dippy conversations that didn't make much sense but didn't need to. Later, she told me she'd had two glasses of champagne before I'd come there, but I never drank, so why was I so giddy?

We were standing there teasing each other, touching each other, when she suddenly grabbed me and put her lips against mine, these soft, wet lips.

"Hey," I said, "what're you doing?"

"Putting on a show for your friends," she said.

Nick and Allie had come out into the hall on their way to the bathrooms. They'd glanced at us but kept right on walking.

112

Huguette grinned up at me. "Did we shock them?"

"Is that what we want to do?"

"Why not? It's your birthday. Do you go to school with them?"

"With her. He's my best friend."

"And Alex is what?"

"I haven't known Alex as long as I've known Nick."

"Oh. Alex is a new friend, then."

"Huguette?" Cog Wheeler had come out into the hall, sunglasses on his head, brown eyes fixed on her.

"If you say my name *You*gette," she told him, "you get *nothing*!"

He liked that.

He laughed, his eyes shining, his hair fire red.

"How about joining the party?" he said to her.

"Are you the party?"

He crooked his arm for her to take and she took it.

I watched her go.

The bathrooms in Roundelay were like the enormous ones in hotels. There was a men's and across the hall a women's.

I'd forgotten Nick was headed there. We hadn't really talked since I'd arrived, just small talk. I didn't feel at all like talking, either, but there he was.

"Hi, Nick."

"I can't believe I'm in the same house with The Failures! This is big-time, buddy! How come you rate?"

"I'm as surprised as you are."

He was drying his hands. I went over to the urinal and unzipped.

"Don't you return calls anymore, Lang?"

"I was going to call you tomorrow." I could still feel her lips on mine, and I remembered how warm her breath was near my mouth.

He was combing his hair although it was already combed.

He said, "Was that some kind of a joke . . . what you told Brittany?"

"No."

"Because it really upset her, Lang."

"We weren't a couple. I kept trying to tell her that."

"She said you told her you and Alex were a couple."

"That's right."

"So you and that French girl *aren't?*"

"No."

"You could have fooled me."

"She has a guy back in France."

"Lots of luck to him."

I zipped up and went over to wash my hands. I'd been planning this moment for a long time, but now that it was here, I couldn't remember anything I'd intended to say.

I said, "Maybe we can talk tomorrow?"

"I'm going out to Montauk. Let's talk now. If what you told my sister is really true, when did you plan to let me in on the news?"

"I wanted to tell you." I took one of the linen towels piled by the washbasin and began drying my hands.

"I don't give a damn if you really are gay, Lang, but I just wonder how come you've never mentioned it to me."

"It's not an easy thing to tell someone."

"Am I just *someone*? Geezus, we've known each other since we were kids!"

"I know."

I wanted to get out of there and go back to the party. There was only one person I wanted to get back to and I knew it. I didn't even care that what we were talking about and what I was feeling were like two and two making five. I could feel the small blue Tiffany box in my pants pocket.

"Why lie to me?" Nick asked me.

"I never have."

"There are lies of omission, you know. If you act one way but are really another way, you're lying."

"Okay," I said. "I lied. I'm sorry!"

"So you're going to leave it at that?"

"This isn't the last chance we'll ever have to talk, is it?"

"What are you mad at?" he said. "I'm the one who should be mad! My sister comes home and springs this thing on me. You don't return my calls. The next thing I know I see you kissing this nearly naked girl out in the hall! Really going at it! Was that an act for my benefit?"

One of the guitarists with The Failures came banging through the door.

I said, "It wasn't an act."

"I didn't think so."

"I mean, it wasn't for your benefit."

I knew I wasn't making sense.

The guitarist stared at his reflection in the mirror and said, "Here sucks!"

He had baggy clothes on a skinny frame, Lyle Lovett hair, and a purple dragon tattooed around his biceps.

Nick said to him, "Hey, you're Lennie Allen!"

"Am I?" was his spacey answer. He was wearing a black Failures T-shirt, splashed with a huge white circle and the word *zero* underneath it.

Nick laughed hard and said, "You're great, man, just great!"

I left.

I couldn't find her.

Then I saw the three of them sitting out on the deck, under a beach umbrella, in the rain. Cog Wheeler, Nevada, and Huguette.

Some little girl with raccoon eyes and breadstick legs cornered me.

She asked me what my instrument was, what my sign was, what song of The Failures was my favorite.

She asked me who was out on the porch I kept staring at.

TWENTY-THREE

We were the last ones left.

The Failures had roared away in their cars, as had Nick, Kevin McCaffery, and the rest. My mother had left with Franklin. Nevada was upstairs in bed.

Huguette sat beside me on a green-and-yellow sofa, holding a glass of champagne. "My third," she said, "so am I a little tipsy?"

"Are you?"

"But I want you to hear 'Paint Over It.' I turned off all the speakers but this one. It'll play next."

"Heart in My Mouth" was playing softly. I remembered the day Brittany had sat up so straight down on the beach and sung the words.

I was trying not to think about Nick. He'd left without saying good night.

"Did you like your party?" Huguette asked me.

"Yes. Thanks again."

"Cog calls you Cloud. He says when you walk into a room, you look like a sudden dark cloud on a good beach day."

"Cog could use some Clearasil."

"What's that?"

"Pimple lotion. For his neck."

Huguette threw her head back and laughed. "You have a vendetta for him, hmmm?"

"He thinks he can have any girl he wants. They all do, those rockers. There's stuff out in your refrigerator that lasts longer than their relationships."

"How long do yours last?" she said.

I shrugged.

"Do you have one?"

I didn't answer.

This was the time to tell her the truth, but the truth was like some porch light on a windy, foggy night: Now you see it shining, now you don't see it at all.

"Hey, here it is now. Listen, Lang. This is Cali."

She had this soft, breathy voice with a sweet ache in it, not bad, not good.

> *Paint over it.*
> *Paint over it will*
> *Never look like new again*
> *Will never get you through again,*
> *But you can still get use from it,*
> *You can just get used to it,*
> *Pick a darker color, too,*
> *So nothing of the old comes through*
> *Paint over it.*
> *Paint over it.*
> *Nothing of the old comes through,*
> *Pick a darker color, too,*
> *Paint over it.*

"She's not great," said Huguette.

"I like the song, though."

We were sitting there with the huge portrait of Nevada glaring down at us, the lights low in the enormous room, the ocean roaring outside, and the rain riddling the windows.

She put her hand on my knee. "I wanted you to hear it. When I'm gone back to Aniane, and you have your car keys"—she giggled—"without having a car"—and then looked into my eyes very gently—"you'll remember sitting here on this kind of wet night out, hearing it for the first time."

"I'll remember this night, anyway."

"So will I, Lang. We've become good friends."

"Maybe more."

"More than friends?"

"Something besides just friends."

She shook her head. "Friends is enough."

I said, "Are you going to see Cog again?"

"Of course I will."

"You *will?*"

"Of course, because Uncle Ben is giving the party tomorrow."

"I thought that was just a ruse to get me here."

"And besides, I really like Cog."

We sat there silently a moment.

She said, "You don't really care about that, do you?"

"Honestly? I think I do."

She said, "If you're speaking *honestly*, I don't think you do. Not that way. Not a jealous way. Back in the hall when I kissed you? I was putting on an act for your friends. . . . You knew that."

She took my hand.

I could feel my heart beat faster. I could feel a way I'd never felt with any girl.

She said, "If we're true friends, you don't have to pretend feelings with me just to flatter me."

"I'm not pretending."

"I think you are, Lang."

"I wouldn't lie to you."

She let out a hoot. "You wouldn't lie? Oh, Lang. From the very first hello you've lied." She let go of my hand. "I told you everything about Martin. And I was waiting for you to tell me about you and Alex."

I couldn't look her in the eye. I couldn't think of anything to say. Plato had come downstairs, and he was standing in the doorway staring at us, wagging his tail.

She said, "Uncle Ben told me all about it, Lang. He said you'd tell me yourself sometime, and I waited."

And punctuating that, with perfect timing, Nevada's voice came from the staircase around the corner. *"Penner? Your birthday was over an hour ago! Go home! Plato! Get back up here!"*

Huguette stood up. "Yes, go home now, Lang."

I went.

TWENTY-FOUR

Fourth of July morning, Franklin's voice came over the intercom in the cottage. "Lang. Fed Ex has a package for you down at the gate. You have to sign for it."

I threw on the top to my pajamas.

"Are you going down there like that?" Mom said.

"Who's going to see me? Franklin's the only one around."

I slipped into my loafers and headed down the road.

The rottweilers had been fed about an hour earlier. I'd heard them barking the way they did when the Range Rover pulled up. I'd heard Nevada take off down Ocean Road after.

I knew the package was probably from Alex.

I was signing for it when the sleek white Porsche pulled into the driveway, top down.

"Hi, Lang," said Cog Wheeler.

I mumbled a hello.

He had on a silk shirt that matched his hair color perfectly. He was waiting for the gate to open, and I imagined the scene Huguette was probably viewing right that moment on the TV.

Cog with success written all over him; me with my hair still tangled from sleep, in pajamas that cried out, "Attention, Kmart shoppers!"

The gate opened, and with a wave of his hand he went up to Roundelay.

I trudged back to the cottage, looking at my watch as I went, wondering what that was all about. A breakfast date?

I sat down on the couch and opened the package.

I'll call you at 11:30. Happy Birthday. I love you, Spartacus. A.

His note was paper clipped to a blue folder.

Horoscope for Lang Penner, prepared by Madam Rattray.

"What's that?" Mom asked.

I held it up.

"What a great gift. See what it says for today."

I had to get past pages of interpretation on the position of the planets and houses when I was born.

The forecast came at the very end.

"It's monthly, not daily," I said.

"Read what it says for July."

I read it:

Your bent to embroider on reality, though done in all good faith, may make you distrusted. You may find yourself "out on a limb." You are competent, however, and your fast reflexes may allow you to extricate yourself from embarrassing situations.

My mother chuckled. "Your fast reflexes? You've been

dragging yourself around like an old turtle this morning."

"Maybe I stuck my neck out when I shouldn't have," I said.

She went back to the kitchen, and I sat there trying to remember how that conversation with Huguette had ended . . . before Nevada called down.

I could hear her saying, "From the very first hello you've lied."

I got up and looked out the window at the kind of perfect summer day there always seems to be after a heavy rain.

Through branches of green leaves under an early-morning sun, I saw the Porsche come back down from Roundelay. Huguette was beside him in the front seat.

Then the phone rang, and Kevin McCaffery told me he didn't expect me to report to work that night.

"You don't want help with the party?"

"Nevada says you're invited to be a guest at the party."

"I don't know about that," I said.

"Suit yourself. Just show up as usual tomorrow when The Failures open. It's going to be a madhouse here. You got that?"

"I got it," I said. "I'll be there." But I didn't mean at the party.

TWENTY-FIVE

I spent that Sunday chopping wood and stacking it while Mom went to church and then off to the Fourth of July celebration in Montauk with Franklin.

I napped and woke up at nine P.M., made myself a sandwich, and tried to watch *The Agony and the Ecstasy* on Bravo. Alex and I would have cracked up at Rex Harrison asking Charlton Heston, "You dare to dicker with your pontiff?" But the line wasn't funny without Alex around. Funny movies weren't funny without him beside me to watch them.

I decided to do the unpardonable: take a walk along the beach, in front of Roundelay. The party for The Failures would be just beginning. Only the chows were home up there.

I wanted to think about what had happened between Huguette and me; mainly, what had gotten into me?

I took a flashlight, although I didn't need it. The moon was full. The sky was lit up with fireworks from Main Beach.

When I reached the sand, I left my loafers behind and headed down toward the hard edge by the water.

What I thought I felt mostly was embarrassment. I walked along imagining what I would say to Huguette next time I was with her. I planned to use my mother's old remark: that coming out was like spilling a glass of wine at a dinner party. But I could almost hear Huguette telling me off: yelling that I'd owed it to her to be as honest with her as she'd been with me.

I was inventing things to say and crossing them out as soon as I thought of them, when I saw someone coming toward me.

Then I saw the chows romping up on the soft sand . . . and then he saw me. His flashlight hit my face.

"Penner?"

"Yeah."

I waited for him to order me off "his" beach.

He turned the flashlight off and stood facing me.

"Why aren't you at Sob Story?"

"Why aren't you, sir? It's your party."

"I don't like those parties in public."

"I don't either."

We began walking back toward Roundelay.

I thanked him for the birthday party, and he grunted something about it being Huguette's idea, not his.

"She's grown very attached to you," he said.

I didn't know if they'd talked since he'd told me to go home; I didn't know what he knew.

I said, "I like her, too. A lot."

"Have you told her about yourself yet?"

"I didn't have to, thanks to you."

"I don't think you ever intended to tell her."

"I did. I was waiting for the right time."

"Bullshit, Penner!"

"Well, she knows now. What's the difference?" I knew what the difference was, but I didn't feel like arguing the point.

"I didn't want her wondering why you weren't champing at the bit to date her," he said. "Thanks to Cog Wheeler, there's someone who is. He's been with her all day."

"I wouldn't call him the ideal someone."

"Maybe he doesn't appeal to you, but he does to her."

"I don't mean that. He might be appealing but he might not be a good choice."

"Why? He's a nice boy!"

"Maybe . . . maybe not. She hasn't had much experience with a fast-track type like that."

"She hasn't had *any* experience. I like Cog."

"I remember you growled at me one morning, 'What kind of a name is Lang?' So what kind of a name is *Cog*?"

Nevada snorted. "He made that up. The cog in the wheel. That's what his father always made him feel like! Oh, I know *that* feeling. Cog and I have a lot in common."

"I didn't realize you knew him."

"I don't *know* him, but I know we're alike. I read an interview with him in *Rolling Stone*. It could have been me talking, twenty years ago!"

"So that makes him a good choice for Huguette?"

"What does *that* mean?" he growled.

"Nothing," I said. I could see the lights of Roundelay. Firecrackers exploded like machine guns.

We walked along without talking for a while, Plato dancing ahead of us, the other chows running scared with their tails between their legs.

"Things are different today," Nevada said. "When we went on the road, all we needed was some penicillin and a little black book. The young fellows today pack laptops, mobile phones, modems; they're real little businessmen."

"Yeah," I said sarcastically.

"You want to argue the point with me, is that it?"

"I wasn't thinking about the difference in equipment on the road," I said. But I wondered what the hell I was trying to prove, why I didn't just shut up and let him think what he wanted to about Wheeler.

Nevada said, "You *do* want to argue it with me. All right, come up to Roundelay and we'll discuss it."

"I can't," I said.

"Stand up for your opinions!" he said. "You throw some out and then back away! You have trouble standing up for yourself, don't you?"

"Maybe sometimes," I said. "But that isn't why I can't come to Roundelay."

"Why can't you?"

"Because Alex is going to call at eleven thirty," I said. "It's eleven ten."

"Just as well, Penner," he said, as we took the path leading up to the house. "I never should have started calling you Penner. You name something, and the next thing you know, you've invited it into your house."

I laughed. "Maybe you should just call me F. I could be the sixth rottweiler."

"You're not fierce enough!" he said. "Plato? Aristotle? Socrates! *Come!*"

I found my shoes where I'd left them, then headed away while he dealt with the chows.

TWENTY-SIX

"You're not going to believe who's playing Cherie," Alex said. "Nola Leary!"

"Who's she?"

"Remember the one in *Picnic* who said she couldn't get excited about kissing an actor who'd rather kiss another male than a female?"

"Oh, no!"

"Oh, yes . . . and she's the director's pet."

"But didn't she know they were casting you?"

"When I got there, she did."

"How's she reacting?"

"We all went off to see the fireworks. So far so good. They were so relieved to get *anyone* at the last minute, I guess she's resigned to having me play Bo. For now, anyway."

We talked about my birthday party, the horoscope, his room, others in the cast, everything but Huguette. He didn't mention her and I didn't.

The moment I heard his voice, any leftover confusion I had from the night before went. I just wanted to be with him. Feel him close, and smell the patchouli.

"Alex? Listen. I'm working some extra hours for McCaffery tomorrow. I think I could get next weekend off. I could fly up Friday."

"That'll cost you plenty, Lang!"

"I've been working for Nevada, too. I have money saved. It'll be worth it if I can just spend a little time with you."

"I'm dying to see you, Lang, but not yet."

"Why?"

"I just explained why. This is a very small town. It'd be hard to get off by ourselves. We're all in the same boardinghouse, one room right next to the other, and no place to go after the show but one beer joint. . . . I don't have a car, either."

"I see."

"Do you see? I'm going to look around and maybe find another place. I don't know what's available."

"Damn! I was hoping we could be together, Alex!"

"Don't," he said. "How do you think *I* feel? Everyone up here is straight as a ruler!"

"That never bothered you before."

"How come it doesn't bother you? You wouldn't even come backstage in New York. What's happened to you suddenly?"

"I miss you."

"I know. I'll think of something. Call you tomorrow."

"I love you," I said.

He said, "You usually don't say that before I do. Absence makes the heart grow fonder, hmmm?"

"Yes," I said, and I hoped it was true.

TWENTY-SEVEN

Except for glimpses of her in the distance, I didn't see Huguette for a week.

Then one morning, when I was repairing the fence around the pool, she called me up to the porch.

"Have lunch with us," she said.

"Okay. Thanks."

I didn't have to ask what band was playing over the speakers. I'd been hearing nothing but The Failures coming from Roundelay all week, whenever Huguette was there.

They'd broken records at Sob Story, sold out every night, six hundred dinners in three days, never mind what the bar took in.

Days I'd see the white Porsche coming and going from Roundelay, often with her beside him. On The Failures' opening night she sat in front at his table. From the kitchen I watched him dedicate his first song to her: Sting's old one, "Every Breath You Take."

Now they were gone, playing a gig in New Jersey.

Huguette had on a long, yellow Failures T-shirt, a version of the one I'd seen on Lenny Allen, with the white circle and the single word *zero*, THE FAILURES stamped across the back. Her black shorts barely showed. She was barefoot and tan.

I sat down and pulled my trouser pants out of my

socks, which I kept up to protect myself from ticks when I worked around the fields.

I couldn't look at her too closely. All the feelings I'd been pushing away for seven days came flooding back.

She said, "Look what he gave me, Lang!"

It was a small, gold identification bracelet.

"He had something engraved on the back," she said. She undid it and handed it to me.

If you say my name Cog, you get Cog.

I gave it back to her.

"The engraver's getting rich this summer," I said.

I never carried the key chain. Nobody had ever given me jewelry with something printed on it before. I was afraid I'd lose it.

"Nobody ever gave me something engraved before," she said. "I'm afraid I'll lose it."

"I know what you mean."

"You know how I always say if you say my name *Eu*gette, you get—"

I cut her off. "I got it," I said.

"He said he might even write a song about it."

"What about Martin?" I said.

"I love Martin." She was fastening the bracelet to her wrist. "This is different. It's just an innocent flip."

"A *fling*," I said.

"Cog's a big star! What would he want with me? He keeps saying he wishes I'd go someplace with him, far away from Roundelay."

132

"I *bet* he would," I said.

"Don't sound so cynical. How's Alex?"

"Busy."

"When will you see him again?"

I shrugged. "Who knows?" Early that morning he'd called me to say he thought he might have a room a few miles from where he was. He might be able to rent a bicycle. There was a possibility that Scotty Lund and Maggie would drive up from New York, the first weekend in August. Maybe I could hitch a ride with them.

"Remember Scotty?"

"Won't that nellie queen ruin your scene?" I'd said.

Alex had said, "You just don't get it, do you? Nobody cares about what kind of friends I have. Everybody knows Scotty. That's different!"

"What would you do with me around? Find me a beard, too?"

"You'd look like a friend of theirs. . . . Lang, Nola Leary is a real bitch! This is an *unusual* situation!"

Then he'd asked about Huguette. I told him she was busy with Cog Wheeler.

Alex had laughed. "You're traveling in powerful circles, love. Don't let it go to your head."

I'd said, "I'm not traveling at all. I'd like to, if you could figure out some way for me to do it!"

"I *hear* you," Alex had ended the conversation. "And I love you! Just hang in there awhile longer, okay?"

❖

Nevada strolled out on the deck, nodded at me, and said, "Penner," then stood a second or so listening to the music.

"That's a bizarre percussion jam tacked on at the end of this," he said. "I'm surprised at Cog."

"Why did he want to talk to you this morning, Uncle Ben?"

"Maybe after an hour he got tired of talking to you," said Nevada. He sat down at the table, across from me. "I think I'll buy some telephone stock if this keeps up."

"What did he want?" Huguette persisted.

"He wants me to come out of retirement." Plato had followed him from the house with a chew stick in his mouth. He sat by Nevada's chair gnawing on it.

"Well? What about it?" Huguette said.

"I have to think about it. It wouldn't be anything permanent. They're doing a gig at The House of Stars in Boston this August. I opened there twenty-three years ago in August. I got my start there." He lit a cigarette while we waited for the rest. Blew a smoke ring. Shook his head. "Cog wants me to walk out and do a number with him. Surprise, surprise sort of thing . . . for sentimental reasons. No advance publicity, no big deal."

"Oh, Uncle Ben—*do* it!"

"I don't know."

I was watching her. I was thinking how easy she'd made it for me to get back with her: no mention of anything that had happened on my birthday night. No need to talk it into the ground, explain, apologize.

What I'd feared most—her asking me what I'd meant when I'd said that maybe we were more than friends—was just passed over. All of it was.

All of it except that strange pull I felt taking me closer to her: not just in my head, but running up and down my arms when I looked at her, as though the blood in my veins was jumping in time with the fast thumping of my heart.

While she talked with Nevada about Cog Wheeler's proposition, I scratched Plato's head and made myself stop watching her. I looked out at the ocean. I thought of Alex's idea to have me go up to the Cape with Scotty Lund and Maggie. I thought of the day on Roosevelt Island when I'd met them, when I'd said there was no such thing as a bisexual.

"Where the hell is our lunch?" Nevada yelled suddenly.

"I'll see what Franklin's up to," Huguette said, and she left me there with him.

"What do *you* think, Penner? You think I should come out of my closet?"

"I'm all for that," I said.

"Out of retirement and back into the fray, just for one night?"

"Sounds good to me."

"It'd be a change," said Nevada. "I miss changing. About all I've changed lately is my clothes. You, at your age, have all your changes ahead of you. Once they're behind you, you're as stuck as a mouse on one of those glue pads we've got down in the cellar."

Aristotle and Socrates came out and joined the party, while Plato trotted off to the other end of the deck, guarding his chew stick.

Nevada leaned forward and spoke in a low, confidential tone. "I think Huguette is beginning to forget her grape picker. Now she knows she can do a lot better than that. . . . And Cog is a good kid. He doesn't drink. He's not on dope."

"How do you know that?"

"I've made some inquiries. Everyone says he's clean, a real businessman. He makes the deals, the decisions. He went to Bush, this very fine school in Seattle." Nevada was in awe of anyone who attended prep school or college, or even someone who took a home-study course in embalming.

He said, "I like his writing. His songs mean something. They remind me of the good writers, the old ones: Joni Mitchell, Simon and Garfunkel." He laughed and added, "Ben Nevada . . . Of course, I suspect he's more interested in Huguette than he is in getting me up to Boston with him."

"Probably both," I said.

"Before the Rochans changed her name, she was called Phoenix . . . after the bird that rises from the ashes. Cali must have felt that everything she did

136

before the baby was destructive. I couldn't help Cali. Her sister said as much; no one could help Cali . . . but now I *can* do something for this child, and it's my only agenda. The Boston thing is just icing on the cake."

TWENTY-EIGHT

In the weeks that followed, I was as much at home in Roundelay as I was down in the caretaker's cottage. I no longer needed an invitation to go up there. I tooted around in the Aurora whenever I felt like it. I was integrated into Nevada's life—a house dog with a pet name.

It seemed as though I spent all my free time up there. Or I drove into East Hampton with Huguette, waited while she phoned Martin, and after listened to her agonize about all the attention from Cog: his nightly calls, his gifts of flowers, candy, and balloons.

If my mother noticed what was happening to me, she didn't question me about it. I think, like Nevada, who began to believe he had turned Huguette down another path, my mother clung to the hope that Huguette was making me forget Alex, and that Mom had been right all along to tell me it was too soon for me to decide that I was gay.

I was in another world at Roundelay, and Alex was firmly entrenched in his world: the theater. He'd never managed to get that room miles from the boarding-house they all lived in. He said that up there, in season, there weren't any rooms he could afford. And anyway, he said, he would be back in New York in six weeks.

The reviews had been excellent. He'd been singled

out as a new young actor to watch. So had Nora Leary. They were getting along okay. He was afraid to rock the boat, so less and less did we talk about seeing each other in August. I wasn't pushing it myself anymore. I sometimes wondered if it was because I knew that summer would be all I'd have of Huguette, that I had never known anyone like her and probably never would again.

Boston may have been only "icing on the cake," as Nevada had put it, but it took precedence over everything. When Nevada wasn't trying out new material on us, he was studying the performers on MTV as though he was taking a crash course in today's rock. He would rage against most of what he saw, criticize and complain, but behind it all we knew he was afraid he would not be well received. Sometimes he said as much, calling himself an "old dinosaur," and the gig "a suicide run."

One hot day near the end of July, Huguette and I took a picnic down to Main Beach. Roundelay was filled with Nevada's arranger, his agent, his tailor, and various advisors helping him plan his appearance at The House of Stars. We wanted to get away from all the activity. She'd never hung out at Main Beach, which was crowded with kids our age: swimming, surfing, playing volleyball.

We walked down a little distance from all that, put up an umbrella, and spread a blanket on the sand.

Cog had called that morning. He said he'd written

a song called "You Get Nothing." He was going to try it out in Boston, the same night Nevada would appear with him. Huguette couldn't stop talking about it.

"I'm a bit dazzled by him, aren't I, Lang?"

"Yes."

"Did you ever feel that way? Feel so happy just having someone new in your life?"

"Yes."

"I know it's hard for you to talk about things."

It never used to be. But it was hard for me to talk about being "a bit dazzled" when she was the one dazzling me.

I said, "And you feel guilty, too." I did. Not just because Alex had no idea how close I'd become to her, but also because for the first time I felt in sync with the ones who'd taken the road most traveled by. I was in disguise as a straight, basking in all the warmth of a world welcoming us with open arms. Huguette and I looked like a couple. Not only was I passing, I was having a good time doing it.

Huguette said, "I *don't* feel guilty. Martin is still the only one for me. Were there others before Alex?"

"No. I had crushes on guys. I never did anything about them. Alex is my first."

"Your first what?"

"Love."

"Finally you say it. Good . . . I know it's different for you. You probably can't talk to everyone about it. But I hope you can talk to me."

140

"I can. Do you think Cog has other girlfriends?"

"He says he doesn't have time."

"Do you believe that?"

"Why would he lie to me?"

"Does he know about Martin?"

"He's very jealous of Martin. He says I'm the kind of girl he could fall in love with."

"I bet Martin doesn't know about Cog."

"He does so. But he's not a jealous type. He tells me that this trip is good for me. This morning he asked me if I'd ever thought of going to school here, and he said that if I did, he'd understand. I told him: Don't be too understanding or I'll think you don't love me enough. . . . But that's Martin. I think he worries some that I haven't seen enough of the world."

I moved out of the sun under the umbrella. She asked me if I wanted her to put some Bain de Soleil on my back. I nodded and felt her hands cool against my skin, kneading my shoulders.

I finally worked up the courage to ask her what I'd been wanting to ask her for weeks. "How far did this thing go with you and Cog? Did you—" I was fumbling for a delicate way to pose the question.

"Did I what?"

"Sleep with him?"

She laughed. "I wouldn't get much sleep, I don't think."

She put the cap back on the tube of suntan lotion

and we sat side by side, watching kids catch the big waves on their surfboards.

"I've never even made love with Martin," she said. "Not the whole thing."

"Really?"

"Surprised?"

"Yeah, I am."

"But *you* have with Alex."

"Sure."

"Only Alex?"

"I told you. Yes."

"Aren't you afraid of AIDS?"

"Of course. But we're very careful. And neither of us plays around."

"I hate that expression!" she said.

"I guess I do too. Or the idea behind it."

"But what am *I* doing to poor Cog?"

"I wouldn't worry about Cog."

She chuckled. "The Cloud speaks."

"Cog can take care of himself."

"You don't even know him," she said.

"I don't have to."

"Oh, Lang, he's not what you think. He's very serious about me. I feel that, even though he doesn't say he loves me. He keeps asking me to come away with him. It's very flattering . . . but what am I doing?"

"Well, you never met anyone that famous . . . and with his own Porsche, too."

"Don't be sarcastic. I never met anyone, famous or not. Aniane is not a hot spot."

"So coming here was good for you, wasn't it?"

"I'll never admit that to my folks. They're always debating about moving back here one day."

"Would you, if there wasn't a Martin?"

"There *is* a Martin. . . . I just don't want anyone to get hurt, Lang."

"Or get hurt yourself."

"Or get hurt myself. Yes . . . I'm a little mixed up, aren't I?"

"A little?" I grinned at her. "You're a mess."

She punched my arm. Hard. Then pushed me backward.

She got up and ran, and I got up and ran after her.

We went down the beach fast, in the sun, laughing.

Finally, I caught her. We wrestled ourselves down to the sand. I held her under me and said, "Say uncle!"

"What?"

"Say uncle!"

She didn't know the expression. She said, "What's Uncle Ben got to do with it?"

I began tickling her and she kicked up sand. We were both laughing and tumbling around. Then I knew I had to roll off her—fast.

I lay on my stomach and she stretched out beside me on her back.

We were both sweating, both out of breath.

"Mon dieu!" she said.

I stayed on my stomach. I had to.

She said, "What would I do without you?"

"Same here," I said.

Sometimes you don't know how happy you are until later when you think back. But I knew then.

I had this sweet longing for her.

It was different from any feeling I'd ever had with Alex, because from the beginning with him, I always knew what would happen next.

With her there was no next, and it didn't matter.

I think we both fell asleep. Maybe she was just being very still while I dropped off for a few minutes.

When I woke up, we were on our sides, turned toward each other. She opened her eyes and smiled. She reached out and drew her fingernail down my cheek. "Do you think the gulls got our lunch, Lang? We'd better go back to the blanket."

"Let them have our lunch."

"What are you thinking, Lang? You look so solemn."

"I think I love you." I just blurted it out.

"No, you don't. You know what you love?" She put her finger between my teeth. "You love to tell lies."

I bit her finger gently. "No. I think it's true."

"If it's true," she said, "then feed me. I'm hungry." She poked her finger into my chin. "Come on!"

I got up and reached down to help her to her feet.

A voice said, "I thought it was you."

I shielded my eyes against the sun and looked up at a girl sitting with a fellow on a blanket behind us.

"Remember me?" Brittany Ball said.

TWENTY-NINE

In the car, on the way home, Huguette babbled on about what I must have done to make Brittany throw the sand cast at me.

"Your friend Nick introduced her to me the night of Cog's party at Sob Story. She was very cool to me."

"She was mad at me, not you. Nick probably told her we were making out the night before at Roundelay."

"Did you tell *her* you loved her, too?"

"Never!"

"No one throws rocks at someone without a good reason!"

"I'd just told her I was gay."

"Ah! It was the other way around with me. First you say you're gay, *then* you tell me you love me."

"I only dated her a few times."

"*Merde*, Lang! She wouldn't be that angry if you hadn't led her on, and *then* dropped the other sock!"

"The other *shoe*."

"The sock, the shoe, you should be locked up." She laughed. "You're a menace."

Huguette's little tirade took the edge off my sudden confession of love. We were both laughing by the time we reached Roundelay.

I drove the Aurora up past the gates and left it and

her in the driveway. I never drove the car to work. I always got a ride with one of the other waiters at Sob Story.

After I finished getting the sand off my feet, then going into the cottage to shower and dress, I was headed down toward the gate when I saw Huguette roar off alone in the Aurora.

My mother told me what had happened later that night after I got home. Franklin had filled her in on the contretemps taking place up in the big house.

Nevada had invited a staff member of The Bentley Academy to drop in at any time, to discuss the idea of Huguette enrolling there.

A Ms. Hamilton was waiting at Roundelay when we'd arrived from the beach.

It was the first Huguette had heard anything about a plan to send her to boarding school in Pennsylvania that autumn.

It was the first she'd heard that her folks were packing up and moving back to New York City. Mrs. Rochan was arriving in New York that Monday to apartment hunt.

"Where was Huguette going in the Aurora?"

"Apparently she went into the village and called that French boyfriend of hers," said my mother. "The Rochans had already told him their plans. And *he* told Huguette that he wanted her to stay here and go to school here."

"How did she take it?"

"You know her. She's a firecracker! She came back to Roundelay and lit into Mr. Nevada."

"I don't blame her," I said.

"I vote with the Rochans," said my mother.

I said, "You always vote with the majority, Mom."

"Don't tell me *you're* disappointed—the way you've been carrying on with her."

"I vote with *her*," I said. "It's a lousy trick!"

That night I couldn't think about anything else. Customers who ordered "Homemade Pot Roast fresh from the oven" were just as liable to get "Our Chef's delicious Fillet of Boneless Chicken Breasts." Red-wine drinkers snapped that they'd ordered white, and vice versa. McCaffery threatened to demote me to dishwasher.

When I got back to the cottage, I walked barefoot down to the beach, watching the lights of Roundelay, hoping somehow Huguette would show up there.

I stayed for hours. Mom woke up when I returned.

"Lang?" she called out to me. "Are you all right?"

"I'm all right."

She knew that I wasn't, knew why I wasn't.

"Those people solve their own problems in their own ways, honey. She'll be okay."

"Yeah," I answered, but I wasn't sure she would be.

THIRTY

"Don't worry about me," she said. "Were you worried?"

I was driving. She was sitting beside me, one hand reaching back to calm Plato, who was on his way to the vet to have a sore paw checked.

"Why do you think I called so early?" I asked her. "Of course I was worried!"

"And Uncle Ben doesn't think Franklin gossips." She laughed. "So you know everything," she said.

"Yeah."

"No you don't. . . . You don't know *my* side of the story."

"What's your side?"

"Stay, Plato! Here's my side," she began.

That was when she told me she wasn't going to Boston with Nevada. Instead, she was going to the Adirondacks with Cog Wheeler on Sunday, after his gig at The House of Stars.

"When Uncle Ben gets back to Roundelay, I won't be there."

I tried to keep my voice calm. Plato was jumping around in the backseat, and she was hollering at him in between telling me all this.

"And then what?" I asked her.

"Uncle Ben will never think of looking for me

there. He'll never think I'm with Cog, either. I told him that if he thought his little plan to fix me up with Cog would work, he was wrong! I said I was never going to see Cog again, and I certainly wasn't going to Boston!"

"He'll find you," I said. "You know him."

"Not for a while, he won't. And before he does, let *him* suffer. I want to hurt him!"

Plato leaped to the front seat.

"I've got him," she said. "He'll sit here on my lap."

"Do you want to hurt me, too? Because you will."

"You'll have Alex. . . . He can't have it both ways, can he, Plato?"

"Get him in the backseat," I said. "I can't concentrate."

"He's all right."

"He's slobbering on my sleeve!"

"The way you thought I would when you called?" She laughed. "You thought I would be all in pieces, but I'm a tough dog too, aren't I, Plato?"

I said, "You don't love Cog, Huguette."

"I want to be with someone who loves me more than I love him."

"You think Cog loves you that much?"

"He loves me more than I love him, because I don't love him to death! I just love him a little."

"Nevada will kill Cog!"

"He won't kill him. And whatever he does do will only be good publicity for The Failures."

I didn't say anything for a while. I didn't know

150

what to say. It was like watching an accident about to happen, like the night in the parking lot when Alex received the first blow and I stood there watching. For a long time after, I kept going over that scene and thinking that I should have done something, helped Alex some way, not just stood there frozen.

She began babbling to Plato, stupid stuff about how they weren't going to be bossed around by Nevada, making the chow pant and drool all the harder.

As we pulled up at the vet's, I finally said, "And what's to stop me from telling Nevada this plan?"

She was attaching the lead to Plato's collar. "You know I'd only make another plan," she said, "so you wouldn't be protecting me, Lang. I don't need anyone's protection!" She opened the car door while she said, "And what about your big feeling for me, huh? Would *you* betray me too?"

I let her go ahead of me, the dog tugging her toward the door. I had to sit there a minute and get control.

She looked over her shoulder at me, that big grin, her hand raised, bracelets jangling down her arm. "C'mon!" she called. "You afraid to visit the doctor?"

A few days later, when I was painting the railings by the gate, Nevada strolled down for a chat. Huguette was up in the pool swimming.

"She's decided not to go to Boston," he said. "Did she tell you?"

"She told me."

"She's disappointed in me right now, but that'll pass. And the scene in Boston is going to be chaotic, anyway. It'll all be videotaped, too. She can watch it someday after she simmers down."

His control over the rottweilers always amazed me. Not a peep out of them when he was on the scene. Before, they'd barked and snarled at me, and A must have lost three pounds charging the fence.

"Poor Cog is bearing the brunt of it," Nevada said. "She won't even speak to him on the telephone." She spoke to him whenever we drove into the village. Her secret calls were to Cog now, instead of Martin.

"She says she wants nothing to do with *any* males." Nevada chuckled. "I guess she doesn't count gay ones. . . . Penner, where did you get that paint?"

"Franklin gave it to me."

"It's too thin. You'll need to do two coats." Then he shrugged. "The thing with Cog wouldn't have worked, anyway. He's too pragmatic. He doesn't have time for a schoolgirl. I think it was Irving Berlin who said the toughest thing about success is that you've got to keep on being a success."

Our "chats" usually went that way, Nevada doing all the chatting. For once I didn't mind. I couldn't look him in the eye, either.

As well as I knew him and what he was capable of doing to get his way, I still felt something for him, particularly at that moment.

Watching him swagger around and mouth off, I could only imagine him later, knees weak from the punch of shock at finding her gone, words hard to come by. It was like watching some tough and arrogant prizefighter in the ring, and being able at the same time to see into the future when he'd get decked and go down for the count.

I never thought the day would come when I'd have Nola Leary to thank for a night with Alex.

"She reserved a room in a motel for her mother," said Alex, "and Mama can't come. And *I* can't wait three more weeks to see you. . . . So I told her we'd take it."

"You didn't tell her *we'd* take it."

"Yes I did, love. She didn't bat an eye. All she said was we were in luck, because she'd made sure it'd be a room on the top floor with a water view. Very romantic, she said. And she said she'd like to meet you. She hoped you'd come backstage."

"Awesome, Alex!"

"Then you will? Can you get the night off?"

"I will! I can!"

"Spend Sunday with me?"

"Yes!"

"And fly back Sunday night . . . unless we can talk them into another night. That way we'd have most of Monday, too."

"Great, Alex! We'll try for Monday, too."

"I can't wait! I miss you!"

"I miss you, too!" I said. "I can't wait either!"

But it was the same weekend Nevada was to appear in Boston, and the Sunday Huguette would leave for the Adirondacks.

THIRTY-ONE

I thought of it as our last date.

I'd purposely asked McCaffery for the whole week-end off, so that Friday night I could take Huguette to Sag Harbor. I got tickets for the Bay Street Theater.

"Let's go whole pig," she said, "dress up and go somewhere fancy for dinner after. My treat."

"Whole hog," I said. "We'll treat each other."

I wore my blue blazer with the gold buttons, a blue T-shirt and white pants, but who saw *me*? People were turning around to get another look at her. I was thinking it would probably be the last time I'd be some-where with someone and get stared at for a good reason. She was decked out in this simple, slinky, way-short silver dress, no sleeves, bare back, no jewelry. Silver pumps with high high heels. Joop.

There were sad songs in the show, the worst kind of sad there is: watching someone leave who won't come back, love-lost themes one after the other.

I thought they'd get to her, make her bawl or make her want to leave—my own eyes filled a few times. But she was not one to wallow in it. She was a fighter, fight-ing back. I didn't know what sad thoughts she was thinking of Martin. I didn't know what qualms she might have had about running off with Cog. We sat side by side, our arms touching, me probably the only one to notice, to feel it beyond the arms. I couldn't concentrate on the play, only the songs. I was thinking my own sad thoughts: that I was losing her, that I was very, very afraid for her, that there was nothing I could do about it . . . was there? I was always thinking, *Was* there?

But I had made her a promise, and I vowed to keep it.

After the play we ate dinner down on the wharf, overlooking the bay. There was a candle lit between us at the table, and a few roses in a tall vase. It was a warm evening, and small boats bobbed in the water at anchor. Some were still out; we could see their distant lights.

She talked about the Rochans some.

"I can't believe my own mother and father would let Nevada manipulate them. He *did* it! He made it possible! They don't have money for a move, for my school. I wouldn't be surprised if Nevada paid Martin off, too!"

"He'd take money?"

"I don't know. His family's very poor, Lang. A big amount of money? Maybe he would. Really, it would be his only chance to own land."

But she didn't dwell on it.

She asked me about what it might be like up on the Cape. I told her I supposed it would look something like Sag Harbor in some places. I told her the plot of *Bus Stop*, and that Alex was playing Bo. I told her about Nola Leary and Alex.

We talked until the candle had burned down and we became aware of the line of people waiting to be seated.

Then we drove back with the sunroof open, stars and a moon above us.

"A perfect evening," she said in the driveway, "and why should it end? Come in. I'll play 'Paint Over It' for you again. You only heard it once."

In the hall the light from the answering machine was blinking.

I went in and flopped down on the nearest couch.

I could hear Cog Wheeler's voice.

"Huguette? Nevada's here. We're hiding him in a suite at The Copley Plaza. I'm having dinner with him there. Listen, love, don't count on Sunday. I can't get away that quickly. Something's come up, love. Where are you tonight? I'll call you in the morning."

Next, Nevada's gruff tone. "You're right to give men up, honey. Cog's got some new flame he only met last night, and they were all over each other while we had dinner here. Do you kids still say 'flame,' or am I dating myself? *Feu*, in French, I believe. This is a side of him I've never seen before. Maybe it's because you dumped him. I'm glad you did. Tomorrow's the big day, honey. I'll think of you. Don't be mad. *Je t'aime.* I'll call you after the show, if it's not too late."

THIRTY-TWO

It was dark outside when I woke up. Plato had jumped up on the bed and burrowed under the covers between us. I still had on my Timex and my T-shirt.

We'd opened the windows to hear the ocean's roar before I'd lain down beside her. "Just for a minute or so," she'd said, "just to hold me." I'd removed my shoes because the coverlet was silk. There was a lamp lit on the table beside the bed. My wallet lay open there, an empty Trojan wrapper next to it.

The only other light was under the huge oil painting on the wall, across from the bed. Nevada and Cali. Although they were dressed seventies style—Nevada in a plaid shirt, jeans, and Converse sneakers, Cali barefoot in a long, flowered dress, her hair spilling past her shoulders—their side-by-side, face-front pose had a formal air. He had one arm around her, the other hand holding up a white rose. She wore no jewelry. Her hands were folded serenely, below her waist. Nevada looked solemn and proud, and she did too, except for the slight trickle of blood from one nostril.

There it was, without explanation. And there I was, with what had happened just as quirky and mystifying.

I lay there remembering how gentle we'd been, how unhurried and calm it had seemed, as though we

158

were floating through some lazy dream that left only this sweet, peaceful feeling.

I smiled, realizing I'd done something I'd never expected I would do, something I'd always imagined I couldn't do.

Then I felt her kick the sheet away.

"Plato, go!" Her voice was angry.

She sat up.

"You go too!" she said.

"What's the matter?"

"What's the *matter*?" She got up, grabbed the silk coverlet, and flung it around her like a toga. "What do you think's the matter?"

"I don't know." I didn't. I sat up.

"You're not gay! You call yourself that?" Her eyes were blazing. "You're a lamp in wolf's clothing!"

"A lamb, a *sheep*," I murmured. "I'm not a light."

"Go home, Lang!"

"It's still the middle of the night. You said you didn't want to be alone."

"I do now!"

I was on my feet, reaching for my clothes.

She said, "I asked you to hold me for a little while!"

"I did."

"You did more!"

"So did you. We both got carried away, I guess."

"Why didn't you stop?"

"You didn't let me, remember?"

I scrambled across the room to get my socks and found just one. I mumbled, "I didn't force you."

"No, you didn't have to, did you?" Her eyes had fire in them. "The other one's under the chair!"

I stuffed my socks into the pockets of my pants.

Socrates was asleep on the floor, my blazer under him.

Plato was back up on the bed, sitting on the pillow, one paw bandaged.

"This didn't happen!" she said.

I stuck my feet into my loafers. "If it didn't happen, why are you so mad?"

She pulled the coverlet around her and glared at me.

She said, "You're like all of them! I thought you were different."

"I thought I was too." I jerked my blazer away from Socrates. I could see the eyes of Aristotle peering out from under the bed.

"I'll never believe anything you say again!" she said. "Not ever!"

"I didn't start it. You did."

She shouted, "I was a wreck!"

"Some wreck," I murmured. "What did you think you were doing? How do you think I felt? I felt—"

She cut me off. "Don't start any sweet talk! Save it for Alex!"

I had my blazer on.

"I'm sorry you feel this way," I said. "I *don't.*"

She laughed scornfully. "Oh, you don't? Of course you don't! And you think that gets you off the hoof!"

I let that one go, but she had another one ready: "You're this big operation, aren't you?"

"*Operator*," I said. "And that's the last thing I am!"

I went out into the hall, Plato limping toward the stairs with me.

She came as far as the banister to shout: "You want to know the *first* thing you are, Lang? You're a liar!"

I walked through the living room with the three sofas, two settees, ten chairs, six benches, and four potted trees.

From the wall Nevada scowled down at me.

I let myself out and stood a moment on the steps, brushing the dog hair off my jacket, glancing at the luminous hands of my Timex. Four A.M.

As I went down the zigzag path, in the fog, I thought of the Red Hot Chili Peppers' old song "Aeroplane." Of Anthony Kiedis singing about having your pleasure spiked with pain. A few times I stumbled and fell, tears just behind my eyes, her words still burning in my ears.

When I got closer to the cottage, I saw that my mother had left the light on for me.

THIRTY-THREE

I flew to the Cape in one of those small planes that never go very high. From my window I could see Long Island disappear, and I wished I could also leave behind the memory of creeping down the path from Roundelay early that morning, like some thief caught red-handed, her angry voice accusing me.

I couldn't forgive Huguette for blaming all of it on me, for not admitting that she'd started it and never tried to stop me. At the same time, my bitterness was mixed with amazement. I knew I would probably never make love that way again. In my mind's eye I saw myself with her there in that moonlit room, both of us suddenly surprised by our own bodies.

It reminded me of dreams I had where I could fly just by waving my arms, how astonished I was that I could do it, how easy it was and strangely graceful.

If she'd only been able to accept what had happened without blame and accusations. If, for once, she'd not become that fiery fighter, forever defending her turf. . . . But then she wouldn't have been Huguette. And I would probably have found myself forced to wonder where we would go from there, what would be next for us.

She knew there wasn't any next.

❖

Alex was waiting for me when I arrived at the small airport. He ran toward me, grinning and waving, hugging me hard.

"Am I glad to see you!" he said.

"Me too!"

I'd never been so glad to see anyone.

One thing I could always count on with Alex, after we'd been away from each other for a while, was that we'd find all the old soft and easy ways we had together again.

I met Nola Leary and others in the cast, and I watched Alex play Bo.

He'd managed to get the room through Monday.

It wasn't until I was on the plane again, flying back to the Hamptons, that I began to look at things in another light. Seeing Alex confirmed what I'd suspected all along: I hadn't undergone some miraculous change. What had happened to me could only have happened with Huguette, could only have come about as it did. We were "firsts" for each other, without ever intending to be. The big difference was, I had Alex in my life and she had no one.

Then I didn't blame her for being angry. I blamed myself for not seeing things clearly. And I felt this urgency to see her, maybe to get the Aurora out and go somewhere away from Roundelay to talk. We'd always been able to talk. She had always taken the lead in our conversations, directed the flow. Now I would. Now I could tell her all I'd felt without making her uncomfortable. And I was aware of the tense in which I'd put that thought: I'd *felt*.

I laughed, imagining her wise-cracking style: *Oh, so now it's felt, not feel, huh? You seduce the girl, then reduce the girl.* . . . Something like that. But she'd be grinning, wouldn't she? She'd be relieved to be off the hoof.

I caught a cab back to the cottage, tossed my garment bag on the chair, and picked up the phone.

"Are you trying to call Huguette?" my mother said.

"Yes. Did she go out?"

My mother nodded, and I hung up.

"She's in New York with Mrs. Rochan," my mother said.

"For how long?"

"She's gone, honey."

"Do you know the number?" I was still standing by the table with the telephone on it, as though I hadn't heard the emphasis she'd put on *gone*.

Mom shook her head. "She said to tell you to read your key chain. I think she must have gotten her English mixed up."

"Not this time," I said. "Was that all?"

"She just said, 'Tell him to read his key chain and tell him I said good-bye.'"

My mother had a way of never prying when she knew something hit me hard. She'd ask me dozens of silly questions about everything going on in my life,

164

but she always let me handle serious personal stuff my own way.

I took a lot of early-morning, late-night walks on the beach after that. I'd watch the sun come up to shine on Roundelay, or the rain come down on the place, or the lights go on. Sometimes my heart would jump when I'd see another person walking toward me through the dawn fog or the darkness, and I'd dare to hope she'd come back.

All the rest of that summer, I could not really believe that she was gone.

But she never returned to Roundelay.

THIRTY-FOUR

I didn't go up to Roundelay after she was gone. I didn't drive the Aurora, either, or do things or go places we'd gone together.

Neither did I ever mention anything about it to Alex. He'd only want to know what it meant, and I didn't want to analyze it, explain it, or name it. Even if I'd wanted to, I don't believe I could have.

Sometimes, not many, I had a few chats with Nevada, mostly about something I hadn't done the way he would have liked it to be done. A few times he tossed in word of her. The Rochans had found an apartment on East Fifty-third Street. She was enrolled at The Bentley Academy in Pennsylvania.

On the day we were moving out, Nevada walked down to the cottage with the videotape of his appearance with The Failures in Boston.

I'd already read an account of it in the *New York Post*. The Failures had been described as "reverently in awe of rock icon Ben Nevada," and Cog Wheeler "nearly dumbstruck by the presence of the higher power, so that he almost forgot to introduce his new song, 'You Get Nothing.'"

Nevada said, "Huguette suggested that you might

like a souvenir." He handed the videotape to me. "I think you're the only good memory she has of this summer."

"Did she say that?" I asked him.

"She doesn't have to. You're the only one she ever asks about."

"What exactly does she want to know?" I persisted.

"Penner, she doesn't want to *know* anything, in particular! If someone says how's he doing, in passing, that doesn't mean she wants to know what you had for dinner last night or what color socks you wore!"

I knew his bark was worse than his bite, but he still made my mother nervous when he sounded off that way. She got the focus back where it belonged: on *him*.

She asked him when he planned to make another appearance.

He shook his head vigorously. "Never!" he barked. "It wasn't a mistake to go back, because if I hadn't done it, I wouldn't know not to do it again. Someone once wrote that the return makes one love the farewell."

I couldn't help putting my oar in. "Well, it got Cog Wheeler a lot of publicity."

"Give him credit: *I* fell for it," Nevada said. "That was what he really wanted. But Huguette saw through him, didn't she? She just dropped him like a hot potato. She learned her lesson with Le Vec!"

Huguette had never told him that it was the other way around; that Cog had dropped her.

167

And if Cog hadn't?

If he hadn't, Huguette and I would probably never have found ourselves together that way.

That night, while Franklin took my mother out for a farewell dinner, I watched the tape.

At the very end, Cog sang the new song.

> *You shouldn't go back if you forgot something*
> *You shouldn't look back if you got nothing.*
> *Lot's wife didn't have a name,*
> *Must be she didn't have a game,*
> *When she looked back she got nothing*
> *If you look back there'll be something*
> *You've got a name (You get)*
> *You've got a game (You get)*
> *You've got a refrain (You get)*
> *"You get nothing"*
> *You'll say it again*
> *And again*
> *"You get nothing."*

Sometimes I'd hear it on the radio, early mornings when I dressed for school. It never made the charts.

One afternoon, when Alex and I were in Venus Records, buying the new Seal album, I got him to listen to it. I told him that Huguette had inspired it.

"You get nothing . . . I remember her saying that to me," he said.

168

"That night we went to Roundelay, yes."

"She was just kidding. Cog Wheeler makes her sound calculating, but she wasn't, was she?"

"No. He was."

"You ended up really liking her, didn't you?"

I said Yes, I'd ended up really liking her.

That fall, Nick asked me once what was with me? He said Brittany had told him she'd seen me down on the beach with the French girl—if that was gay, what was straight?

"And I saw the way you were with her that night of your birthday," he added.

I said, "You should see me with Alex."

"Do I *have* to?" He laughed.

For a while Franklin still looked my mother up when he came into New York. She said she'd never managed to melt that icy exterior; it was like dating Mr. Spock, the gentle but unfeeling Vulcan from *Star Trek*.

The last we heard of Nevada, he was back in seclusion. Franklin reported that things were normal again at Roundelay. Once, Cali's sister, Mrs. Rochan, had visited, but Huguette had stayed with Mr. Rochan in New York.

Afternoons after school and weekends I had a job waiting tables in a small sandwich shop on upper Fifth Avenue. It was a favorite hangout for older teenage girls.

They'd come in carrying shopping bags from Saks and Bloomingdale's, and order rice-milk cappuccinos. Even though I knew that Huguette was in Pennsylvania, I wondered if she came home some weekends. And what would happen if she wandered in one day? What would we say to each other? How would it feel to see her again?

Winter came early that year, with snow already at Thanksgiving.

Alex was busy investigating opportunities in summer theater. Wherever I'd be, I'd have to have a full-time job, because it would be my last summer before college.

Mom was thinking about going into business in June with a woman who had a catering service up on the Hudson, in Piermont, New York.

One night she showed me photographs of the house she'd rent, overlooking the Tappan Zee Bridge.

"Right near Alex's parents' place," I groaned.

"Oh, they're used to you two by now."

"Maybe I'm not used to them."

But I was. Both Alex and I were handling "the slings and arrows" a lot easier.

My mother said, "Rockland County isn't the Hamptons, but I've had the Hamptons. I think of last summer as The Summer of My Wooden Soldier."

I grinned, remembering the novel called *The Summer of My German Soldier.* She'd helped me with the book report I'd done when I was in sixth grade.

I still carried the key chain in my pocket, with

"Paint Over It" engraved on the gold circle. I still remembered one line from the song: *Pick a darker color, too, So nothing of the old comes through.*

I didn't tell my mother my own feelings about that summer. But I knew that it was a time I'd never forget.

I knew that I'd always think of it as the summer that I loved a girl.